"I'll... about me.

Spence felt the impact of her lips and her warm breath in the depths of his soul. "I know you'll be okay." *I plan to make sure you are,* he silently vowed. No one harms you, Viva Conrad. No one. Not ever.

"I'll probably spend most of the weekend resting."

"And eating properly?"

"And eating properly," she promised with a faint smile.

He leaned forward then, unable to resist the sheer temptation of the laughter dancing in her eyes and his memory of the lushness of her lips, lips he needed to taste once more, although he knew he was indulging in a form of self-torture.

"Spence . . . ," she whispered on a sigh.

"That's my name," he answered before he brushed his lips lightly over hers.

Viva moaned, then undulated against him. Caught up in the sensations raging like a brush fire through his entire body, Spence felt his control unravel even more. He surrendered to the heat and hunger driving him, helpless to resist Viva's responsiveness.

WHAT ARE *LOVESWEPT* ROMANCES?

They are stories of true romance and touching emotion. We believe those two very important ingredients are constants in our highly sensual and very believable stories in the LOVE-SWEPT line. Our goal is to give you, the reader, stories of consistently high quality that may sometimes make you laugh, sometimes make you cry, but are always fresh and creative and contain many delightful surprises within their pages.

Most romance fans read an enormous number of books. Those they truly love, they keep. Others may be traded with friends and soon forgotten. We hope that each LOVESWEPT romance will be a treasure—a "keeper." We will always try to publish

LOVE STORIES YOU'LL NEVER FORGET
BY AUTHORS YOU'LL ALWAYS REMEMBER

The Editors

ANTICIPATION

LAURA TAYLOR

BANTAM BOOKS
NEW YORK · TORONTO · LONDON · SYDNEY · AUCKLAND

ANTICIPATION

A Bantam Book / August 1997

ISBN 0-553-44602-9

Published simultaneously in the United States and Canada

Bantam Books are published by Bantam Books, a division of Bantam Dou-
bleday Dell Publishing Group, Inc. Its trademark, consisting of the words
"Bantam Books" and the portrayal of a rooster, is Registered in U.S.
Patent and Trademark Office and in other countries. Marca Registrada.
Bantam Books, 1540 Broadway, New York, New York 10036.

PRINTED IN THE UNITED STATES OF AMERICA

OPM   10 9 8 7 6 5 4 3 2 1

This book is dedicated to
Pat and Bill Klussman,
two very special friends who have
welcomed me into their lives and
introduced me to the remarkable world
of Thoroughbred horse racing.
Sincerest thanks!

ONE

"You've changed," accused the man who stood in the shadow-filled doorway of Viva Conrad's office.

She gripped her pen. Otherwise, she didn't move a muscle. She even stopped breathing for several long seconds.

Viva recognized his voice. She couldn't forget it if she tried—and she had. The resonant sound came back to haunt her in her dreams. It played a part in every fantasy she had of what might have been, had fate not stepped in and threatened all that she held dear.

"It's taken me more than a year to find you. I'm not leaving until we've talked, so don't ignore me."

Ignore Spencer Hammond? Not even remotely possible, Viva realized. He would be a part of the fabric of her thoughts, her heart, and her life until she drew her last breath.

Lifting her gaze from the spreadsheets that littered the top of her desk, she focused on him. She inhaled and exhaled shallowly, her heart racing beneath her breasts. She'd expected him, but she wasn't prepared to deal with him.

He walked into her office, his stride and bearing a testament to his self-confidence. Spencer Hammond, her longtime friend and trusted confidant until the nightmare had begun and she'd done the unforgivable.

She couldn't look away from him. He reminded her of all she'd lost. And he worried her, because he could be relentless when he wanted something.

Giving him what he wanted in this instance, Viva knew, meant she would be jeopardizing his life and the life of his college-age daughter. She refused to do that, although she was thwarting justice and protecting a murderer with her silence. What an unholy mess! she thought to herself.

"I thought I knew you. Shows you how wrong a person can be, doesn't it?" he asked.

His expression assured her that he didn't really expect a reply. She didn't supply one. She couldn't. She wanted to weep, but she maintained her composure instead.

"Tommy's funeral was well attended."

She winced at the censure in his tone, his reference to her late uncle denting her facade of self-control.

"Nothing to say, Viva? No pretense of regret? Perhaps 'I just didn't give a damn' would be a more honest response than 'I'm sorry, I just couldn't squeeze the event into my busy social calendar' or 'I couldn't get a flight home.' "

"Uncle Tommy is at peace now, Spence." She spoke softly, her Kentucky roots evident. "And he's no longer in pain."

"He's dead, dammit, and he died alone."

She searched his rugged features, and she saw the toll the last fourteen months had taken on him. "Nothing will bring him back, but he didn't die alone, because you were with him. You weren't just his business partner, you were his friend."

"Why weren't you there, especially near the end?"

She met his gaze. She remained mute by choice.

"Why, Viva? After all he did for you, how could you turn your back on him when he needed you the most?"

She straightened in her chair, refusing to cave in to the emotions crashing over her like a tidal wave bent on total devastation. The regret she felt at not being at Tommy's bedside dominated her every waking thought.

"I don't owe you an explanation for the choices I've made, Spence. Not now. Not ever."

"You owed Tommy," Spence countered, his voice rife with contempt.

She met his gaze, but she refused to defend herself. She was already defending Spence and his daughter by allowing herself to be manipulated by the death merchant responsible for killing Michael Hammond, Spence's stepbrother and her former fiancé. To guarantee Spence and Emily's survival, she'd agreed to have no contact with Spence, and she'd abandoned her home. In effect, she'd given up the life she loved and started a new one in San Diego fourteen months earlier.

"Tommy took you in when your folks died, gave you a loving home, and raised you in the lap of luxury like some princess in training for a palace."

"He was my uncle, and he loved me," Viva whispered. "He understood."

"And now he's left you the bulk of his estate."

She nodded warily, aware of the pitfalls of having this conversation. Viva took a steadying breath.

"I won't allow you to run away again," he warned.

She sank back in her chair, her fingers knotted in her lap as she projected a calm she didn't feel. "I'm not planning any trips. I have a life here in San Diego, in case you haven't noticed. And, for the record, you don't have the right to give me orders."

He frowned at her. "I've noticed a hell of a lot, Viva. I noticed Michael's so-called suicide fourteen months ago. I noticed that my mentor and partner was dying because his heart couldn't sustain him. And I definitely noticed the absence of the one person those two men had in common, the woman they both adored. Trust me when I tell you that I noticed," he finished.

"Don't try to make a gift of your bitterness, Spence, and don't ever make the mistake of judging me," she cautioned, willing now to defend herself. "I won't tolerate that kind of behavior, not even from you."

He approached her desk, leaned down, and braced his powerful upper body with his hands as he glared at her. "You dropped off the map without a single word of explanation to anyone. You really are a piece of work, aren't you?"

"Get out of my office," she ordered. She pushed to her feet. She resented his intimidation tactics almost as much as she longed to throw herself into his arms and plead for comfort in the wake of more than a year of isolation and loneliness. "Get out now. We have nothing to talk about. Any communication between us can be handled by lawyers."

Spence straightened, his gaze unrevealing as he watched her.

Viva walked to the bank of windows on the far side of the room and turned her back on him. The panorama of twinkling city lights and the advancing bank of night fog sweeping in from the ocean outlined her rigid posture and revealed the control she exerted over her emotions.

"What the hell happened to you, Viva?" he demanded as he shoved ruthless fingers through the thick crop of dark hair that topped his head. "You used to be a caring and compassionate woman. You knew how to put other people's needs in front of your own when it was necessary. You used to feel, dammit. Why did that stop? Why did you disappear? Why are you acting like some bloody ice queen?"

Tears stung her eyes. She blinked them back, refusing to fall apart in front of Spencer Hammond. Never in front of Spence.

"Talk to me," he commanded as he moved across the width of her spacious office in a pediatric medical clinic dedicated to the needs of underprivileged children. He stopped a scant foot from where she stood.

Turning, she looked up at him. She'd forgotten how tall he was. She hadn't forgotten the intensity and force of his personality, however. He rarely ran roughshod over anyone, and only if he'd been pushed to the limit of his endurance. She'd pushed him. She knew that as well as she knew the name of the cologne he wore, his fondness for Irish cableknit sweaters, and his passion for Thoroughbreds. She understood the cause of his anger and frustration, just as she knew that she would never again be the recipient of his trust.

"I have nothing to say, Spence, aside from the obvious. I think you should leave. There's really no point in talking. We have absolutely nothing to discuss."

She knew she was kidding herself. Her inheritance, which she'd been informed of the previous day by Uncle Tommy's lawyer, made conversation between them critical. Why, she wondered, had Tommy put her in this position? He'd known the risks involved, because she'd confided in him on the heels of Michael's death. He'd even facilitated her departure from Kentucky the day after the funeral.

Spence reached out and settled his hands on her shoulders. Startled, Viva trembled beneath his touch. She tried to steel herself against the rush of desire spilling into her veins and weakening her resolve. When she felt the heat from his fingers and palms penetrate the linen fabric of her dress, she wanted to move forward, wanted nothing more at that moment than the feel of his strong body aligned to her own. She ached inside with the effort required to contain the rainbow of emotions coursing through her.

She scanned his face, taking in the angular contours, his strong jaw, and expressive dark eyes. There was nothing pretty about Spencer Hammond. He was all roughly hewn male, and very much a product of his Kentucky heritage and three generations of a family whose lives and livelihoods had been dominated by Thoroughbred horse racing.

He tilted his head to one side, studying her intently and searching, Viva sensed, for the answers he needed. For a brief moment she wondered what he saw when he looked at her. She suddenly realized that she'd become his personal symbol of betrayal and indifference. She trembled, wanting something else altogether from Spencer Hammond, wanting what she couldn't have, wanting him.

Frightened that he might notice the hunger his

touch provoked, Viva wrenched free of him. "I don't like to be handled."

His shock at her behavior showed in his thickly lashed eyes. "What in hell's wrong with you?"

She tried to step past him. He blocked her path, his tall, sturdily constructed body a sufficient barrier to her slender frame and her desire for distance between them.

As they silently regarded each other, Viva feared that he might discern the complex emotions she struggled even now to keep a secret—feelings for him that she would never have the luxury of voicing, feelings that had shocked her when she'd recognized them for what they were, and finally, feelings that had been the catalyst for her decision to end her engagement to his stepbrother.

"Answer me, Viva."

She closed her hands into fists at her sides. "I just told you," she said. "I don't like being handled as if I were a sack of feed."

"You haven't uttered a truthful word since I walked in the door, so why should I believe anything you say now?"

"Thank you, Spence."

Her words were facetious. They both knew it.

"Let's talk about your inheritance, partner," he suggested, his voice like granite.

"Uncle Tommy's lawyer faxed me a copy of his will yesterday. I'm aware of the terms."

"And," he prodded.

"And what? Tommy meant well, but I don't want what he left me."

"You don't want hundreds of thousands of dollars' worth, perhaps millions over the long haul, of Thoroughbred stock? You don't want half ownership in the finest animals on a racetrack this side of heaven? You don't want to be the co-owner of Anticipation? Pardon me all to hell, but I don't believe you."

"Believe it, Spence," she hissed like a cornered feline. She told herself to relax in the moments that followed, and she didn't speak again until she had. "And believe me. I'm prepared to surrender my half of the partnership to you. Right now, as a matter of fact."

"No way," he muttered, his dark eyes narrowing speculatively. "No damn way."

"It would solve all your problems," she pointed out. "You won't have to deal with me, and we both know that you wouldn't mind being in complete control."

"Forget it."

She tried another approach. "If you're unwise enough to reject my offer, then have your lawyer draw up a power of attorney. I'm content to be a silent and nonparticipatory partner. You'll have carte blanche."

"You can't be serious."

Viva knew that a less honorable man would kill for a filly like Anticipation, but not Spencer Hammon. Like his late business partner and mentor, he possessed both honor and integrity. "I've never been more serious in my entire life. I haven't got the time or the desire to take on any additional responsibilities."

"You're lying to me and to yourself. No one with your background and knowledge of Thoroughbreds abandons a front-row seat to or her claim on a three-year-old filly like Anticipation."

"This isn't about money or horses or races," she protested.

"Then what's it about?"

"That doesn't concern you."

"We will project a united front, partner," he told her. "The terms of Tommy's will have been made public by the lawyers for the estate, per his instructions before he died. Everyone expects you to represent Oakbrook Farm. I expect it. The announcement's been made. If you don't, you'll cause speculation and controversy that could undermine everything Tommy and I have worked for during the last ten years."

She knew the horse racing community well enough to realize that he was probably right. "That's unfortunate," she conceded with regret.

"No kidding," he said harshly. "This entire situation's unfortunate, but we're going to make it work."

She shook her head. "I can't become involved." *I can't risk it,* she wanted to shout.

"Tommy's reputation is on the line. He expected you to honor his dreams and become a full partner in this enterprise. It's his legacy, and he's placed it in your hands for safekeeping. I won't let you fail him or tarnish his memory."

"Look, your reputation as an owner is impeccable, so you don't need me. And Ben is one of the top trainers in Thoroughbred horse racing," she pointed out, referring to the man who'd worked with Anticipation since her acquisition by Spence and her late uncle. "If anyone questions my decision to decline my inheritance, tell them the truth. My interests have changed, and I'm happy using my business degree as the administrator of this medical clinic. End of story."

"Forget it. You're a part of the equation now, and I don't intend to let you off the hook. The Del Mar season starts in a few days."

"I don't have a California racing license." Flimsy, she thought even as the words passed her lips.

"That can be dealt with, as you well know. We'll use guest passes while you complete the application process. You'll have to be fingerprinted and undergo a background check, so carve out the time on your calendar. In the meantime, I've reserved a box at the track. Anticipation won't be arriving for a few weeks, but four other partnership horses have already been shipped in from Hollywood Park. We have two more arriving today from New York. Ben has everything under control."

"I have a life," she declared heatedly, "and commitments that I cannot ignore."

He glared at her. "We'll work around all that. Once the Del Mar meet is over, we can sort out the rest of this mess. For now, our goal is to see that Anticipation continues her winning streak, not fight over the conditions of Tommy Conrad's will. I need you, partner, and I expect you to deliver."

Oh, Spence, I wish you needed me in the same way that I need you. She reclaimed her pride and dignity with both hands. "I won't be forced, coerced, or otherwise manipulated, so get that reality into your head and keep it there."

He gave her a troubled look. "You're not making any sense, Viva. All I'm asking you to do is to spend time with friends from home, people who watched you grow up, people who used to mean something to you. Why is that a problem for you?"

Her heart went out to him then. He'd lost his brother and his business partner in the space of fourteen months. She'd spent every day since Michael's death dedicated to safeguarding Spence and his daughter. In the process, she'd failed the uncle who'd given love and a home to an orphaned seven-year-old girl when she'd lost her parents in a tragic car accident.

From Spence's perspective, she was a coward, but he didn't know the gravity of the situation. She was being threatened by a man who was capable of ordering the deaths of innocent people. She knew him to be a paranoid predator, so she took his threats seriously.

How and why, she wondered, had Uncle

Tommy overlooked the very reason she'd fled Kentucky in the first place as he'd determined the distribution of his estate? She couldn't even begin to fathom his reasoning, although she'd spent most of the previous night trying.

Impulsively reaching out, she placed her hand on Spence's forearm. "I'm doing what's best. Please believe me."

His jaw tightened. "You're doing what's expedient for reasons I don't understand. My instincts tell me you've got one hell of a hidden agenda."

She withdrew her hand and moved away from him. "Have it your way." She felt his gaze on her as she walked back to her desk and sank into her chair.

He followed her, then started to pace the area in front of her desk. "What's happened to you?" he asked, the edge gone from his voice.

She smiled, but it was a smile tinged with sadness and regret. "Life."

He exhaled, the sound like a harsh gust of wind. "I want Tommy's dreams realized, Viva, and one of those dreams was his plan to have you take over for him." He paused, shoving his hands into the pockets of his trousers as he stood in front of her desk. "Don't you want the same thing?" he asked.

I want you to live to enjoy your next birthday, and I want Emily to graduate from college, she longed to say. "You're perfectly capable of bringing his dreams and goals to fruition. Look, Tommy meant well. He was the soul of generosity, but this time it was misguided."

"He loved you like his own, Viva."

Tears brimmed in her eyes. Her chin wobbled before she got herself under control. "You aren't telling me something I haven't known all my life, Spence."

"My stepbrother loved you, too, even after you called off your engagement to him."

Exhaling raggedly, she met his gaze. She couldn't have spoken at that moment if her life had depended on it.

"Nothing to say?"

She forced herself to respond. "I couldn't give Michael what he deserved."

Spence remarked, "That's what he told me, but he wouldn't say anything more."

"Our breakup was private. It didn't concern anyone but the two of us."

"I'm having a hard time believing you, especially after reading the note he supposedly wrote."

Viva knew he was referring to the typed letter she found on Michael's desk. She'd given it to the police, even though the contents had been a lie. She'd allowed the authorities to believe that Michael had been despondent over their broken engagement. Her motive, then and now, had been to protect the last two members of the Hammond family from Michael's ex–business partner.

Viva offered, "I'll think about what you've said, and I'll give you a decision within twenty-four hours. That's the best I can do."

"You can reach me at L'Auberge," he told her,

referring to the beachfront resort in Del Mar that he and Tommy had always favored during the racing season.

"I'll call you."

He fell silent for several moments, then asked, "Didn't you miss us at all, Viva?"

So much, she thought, that she nearly died of loneliness. "Yes," she said, barely holding herself together.

"Then why didn't you come home for a visit?"

"I couldn't."

"Why did you leave the day after Michael's funeral without saying a word to anyone? Why didn't you at least call me? We were friends, Viva. Good friends. Didn't that count for anything?"

She hadn't had any other choice, she remembered. "I needed a change of scenery."

He pressed, "The police were certain that you weren't completely honest with them when they interviewed you."

Her heart skipped a beat. She recalled numbly answering the phone at Michael's apartment just after she'd discovered his body. She remembered that the caller had referred to Spence and Emily as his insurance policy. He'd refused to listen to the truth, which was that she couldn't compromise him, because she knew nothing specific about his business deals with Michael. "The police were wrong," she said belatedly.

"Were they?"

Viva paled, but she nodded.

"I don't agree. You know damn well that Michael didn't commit suicide. My stepbrother loved life, and he loved you."

"You have a right to your opinion," she said quietly.

"Am I wrong, Viva?"

"That's not for me to say."

"You know things about that night, don't you? You know things you've kept secret from me and from the authorities."

"Spence, I've had a long day—"

"And I've had a very long fourteen months," he interrupted sharply.

"I know, but I can't change the past. All I can deal with . . . all any of us can deal with . . . is the future."

He switched gears with characteristic adeptness. "Tommy intended for our futures to be linked as partners."

"Uncle Tommy meant well," she said for the second time since his unannounced arrival at her office.

"Then accept his gift."

"I've already promised to give you an answer tomorrow."

"And will you provide other answers?"

"It depends on the questions you ask, Spence."

"I don't know you any longer, do I?"

She sighed, the sound filled with regret and emotional fatigue.

"Michael's death—"

"Stop it, Spence," she broke in. "I'm not going to rehash the circumstances with you, so give it a rest."

"You found him that night. You were barely coherent."

A sudden chill worked its way up her spine. "I found him, and I called the police. I was also in shock. Who wouldn't have been? That's all there was to it."

His expression hardened. "I intend to have the truth, Viva. Before I go home to Kentucky, I'll have it."

She squared her shoulders. "Don't use that tone of voice with me, Spence."

"Just stating a fact, one I suggest you get used to."

"Leave now, Spence. Leave before you say things that can't ever be repaired."

She sank back in her chair as he started out of the room. He paused in the doorway. She pressed her fingertips to the pulse battering her temple.

"Are you all right?"

"Just fine," she said as she fought the emotion swelling in her throat. Peering back at him, she pushed aside the heavy curtain of shoulder-length black hair that had fallen across her cheek with shaking fingers.

"You look exhausted."

So hungry for the tenderness and compassion she heard in his voice, she didn't bother to deny the obvious. "I am."

His gaze roved over her. "You've lost weight since I last saw you."

She shrugged, then glanced away.

"Is there anything you need?"

"No, but thank you for asking."

"You still have Sunday school manners."

She almost smiled. "Momma insisted. Uncle Tommy continued the tradition."

"I may be angry with you right now, but I care about you, Viva."

She didn't know what to say, and her confusion showed in the vivid blue of her large eyes as she looked at him.

"I'm worried about you, little one. You're obviously pushing yourself way too hard these days."

Her heart nearly stopped beating when she heard the endearment he'd always reserved for her. She'd missed it, just as she'd missed the man. "There's no need for you to worry," she whispered.

"Isn't there?" he asked before he turned on his heel and walked out of her office.

Viva sat very still in the minutes that followed. The tears that had threatened repeatedly during her confrontation with Spence refused to fall. Like her emotions and her anxiety for his safety, they remained bottled up inside her.

TWO

Following her second sleepless night in a row, Viva faced the dawn resigned to cooperating with Spence, but on her terms. She knew she'd be walking a fine line between rousing the ire of a napping tiger and blunting Spence's curiosity, but she didn't think she had any other choice.

As she left her bed, donned her robe, and made her way to the kitchen, Viva harbored no illusions about Spence. He would continue to pursue the truth about her reasons for leaving Kentucky, while she endeavored to guarantee his well-being.

She intended to sidestep the media people who covered the Thoroughbred world by pleading scheduling conflicts during the events that took place at high-profile meets like Del Mar. She reminded herself as she absently listened to her coffeemaker gurgle that a calm demeanor and selective socializing would allow her to remain in the background most of the time.

If the one person she truly feared attended the Del Mar meet, she would backpedal to the opposite side of the planet, regardless of Spence's reaction to her behavior. As he'd so bitterly pointed out, she'd dropped off the map once before. Viva knew she could do it again if the need arose.

As for her emotions where Spence was concerned, she doubted that she would be able to conceal them indefinitely. Loving him was both a blessing and a curse, but she decided an aloof facade would forestall the possibility of embarrassing Spence and humiliating herself, at least in the short term.

After filling a mug with coffee, Viva reached for the phone. She jumped when it rang, then answered it on the third ring while simultaneously telling herself to settle down. "Hello?"

"Good, you're awake," Spence said.

"I work for a living," she reminded him tartly, chagrined yet again by his penchant for seizing and maintaining the upper hand in everything he did.

"You sound froggy."

"It's early. I always sound this way."

"I remember," he said, his voice losing some of its edge. "So, did you get any sleep last night?"

He knew her too well, she realized. "I've made a decision."

"The right one, I assume."

"Don't, Spence. I'm not in the mood to be subjected to your highhanded behavior."

"Is that what I'm doing?" he asked.

"I'm not sure what you're doing, and I'm probably better off not knowing."

"I assume you have conditions."

"Of course."

"I'm listening."

She ignored his terseness, understanding the cause and not able or willing to fault him. "I'm prepared to participate in the race season as long as it doesn't interfere with my work. I intend to decline all media requests for interviews. Those are your responsibility. I will attend social functions hosted by people I know," she clarified. "In short, I won't be put on display."

His silence deafened her, but she made herself wait. Turn me down, Spence, she silently begged, and let me walk away from this entire situation.

"Agreed," he said.

Startled, she didn't know what to say now that he'd accepted the limits she'd placed on their partnership.

"Didn't expect that, did you?"

"I'm an eternal optimist."

"So am I. Guess we're well matched, aren't we?"

Emotional fatigue made her sound wary. "This isn't a competition, Spence."

"It's a contest of wills, pure and simple."

She pressed her fingertips to her forehead. "No, it's not."

"Then what is it?"

"I have a final condition," she said, unwilling to answer his question.

"The other shoe has finally dropped."

"Sarcasm doesn't suit you."

"It suits my mood."

"If you act like a bully, I'm history."

He chuckled, but it wasn't a happy sound.

Viva tensed. "You only get one warning, Spence. I have limits, and I don't intend to exceed them."

"You really have changed, haven't you?"

"Real life is fluid, and we all have to adapt," she answered. "You know that as well as I do."

"Then I accept your terms, partner."

"The real question is, will you abide by them?" She waited then for his reply. Once, she might have been willing to justify her intransigence, but not now.

"To the best of my ability."

"Thank you," Viva said, aware that he was the kind of man who always tried to honor his promises.

"I'll be in touch once I have the opening day schedule," he said before severing the connection.

She swallowed a groan of frustration. Touch. He'd be in touch. She wanted his touch. God! She craved it. Unceasingly.

She recradled the telephone receiver and

reached for her coffee, but she hesitated when she saw the way her hand was shaking. A few minutes passed before she risked lifting the mug of coffee to her lips.

The pageantry and fanfare of opening day at the Del Mar racetrack brought out the curious, the veteran handicappers and gamblers, the moneyed elite who financed the "sport of kings," the media, and thousands of spectators who placed modest wagers and fantasized about picking winners.

Brilliant sunshine, balmy ocean breezes, and the music of the strolling mariachi bands added to the festive mood as the day unfolded. Those in attendance delighted in the annual parade of hats, which ranged between ludicrous and genuinely humorous. Excitement hummed in the air prior to the start of each race.

Before the final race of the afternoon, after finishing his conversation with a jockey agent who represented his jockey of choice for Anticipation, Spence paused to study Viva as she chatted with old friends near the railing that encircled the saddling paddock.

There was no denying her beauty, he realized. She was even more exquisite than ever, despite the haunted look that periodically filled her eyes whenever he caught her scanning the crowds. Her wariness, although subtle most of the time, set his nerves on edge, but not nearly as much as the never-ending parade of male admirers she attracted.

Spence couldn't get past his suspicion that she'd dressed for the day with the intention of avoiding recognition. Clad in a pale silver silk suit with matching pumps and shoulder bag, she wore a wide-brimmed hat with a delicately woven veil that covered half her face.

It wasn't that her attire was inappropriate. Many of the women in attendance were elegantly clothed. But the Viva of old hadn't been the kind of woman to make fashion statements. She'd preferred far more casual clothing. This woman appeared remote, even somewhat mysterious. And, he silently amended, drop-dead sexy thanks to her hourglass-shaped figure and legs that seemed to go on for miles.

Spence felt yet another startling surge of desire flood his bloodstream. It wasn't the first time he'd reacted this way to her since arriving in San Diego, and he sensed it wouldn't be the last.

He'd never been more aware of her femininity. In the past she'd occupied the position of close friend. Genderless friend, for the most part. He'd never experienced the kind of desire for her that kindled powerful sexual urges.

Why now? he wondered as he grappled with the need to touch her and taste her at his leisure.

He wanted to explore each and every curve and hollow of her body, and then sink slowly into her softness and bask in the heat emanating from her skin—skin delicately scented by a fragrance that was as mysterious as the woman standing just a few yards away.

He needed to know Viva Conrad in a way that he'd never known her before. Intimately. He felt thrown off balance by the depth of his need and uncertain about how to deal with his longing.

With any other woman his predicament would have been easy to deal with, but not with Viva. What in hell was it about her that made her so desirable all of a sudden?

He shook himself free of the seductive images in his mind and the erotic impulses streaming through him like currents of liquid flame. He reminded himself that Viva was a friend, not a prospective lover. His visceral response to her was his problem, he concluded. God only knew how she'd react if he came on to her. Hell, she'd probably laugh in his face.

Annoyed by the path his thoughts had taken, he strolled toward her, glowering at the men clustered around her. He shouldered his way through the throng, taking satisfaction from the fact that several of the men stepped back a few paces once they noticed him.

Spence paused at Viva's side, met her gaze, and wondered grimly how he was going to get through the next two months. He reached for her hand. "Ready to head back to the box?"

She nodded as she walked past him, neatly avoiding his touch. "Of course."

He frowned at her deliberate sidestep. What had gotten into her? Better yet, what had gotten into him? He was damned if he knew the answer to either question!

"Enjoying yourself?" he asked, striving for a casual tone.

"Very much. It's nice to see old friends."

Spence glanced at her. "You've been gone a long time."

"Too long," she answered.

Her unguarded admission caught him off guard. It also validated his conviction that she was keeping secrets worthy of exploration, for both their sakes. Spence refrained from touching her as they threaded their way through the crowd. "Your friends care about you, Viva."

"I know," she whispered.

She sank into her seat once they reached their reserved box. Setting aside her purse, Viva focused on the activity on the track.

Spence sat next to her. Reaching out, he placed his hand over hers. Viva flinched, but she didn't pull away from him this time.

"What's wrong?" he asked, compassion displacing his annoyance and concern resonating in his low voice.

She shook her head. "Nothing."

"Talk to me, Viva."

She flashed a bright, totally manufactured smile in his direction, then shifted her gaze back to the racetrack. "About what, partner?"

"Your fingers are like ice."

She tried to pull free of him, but he gripped her hands with tempered strength. He didn't want to hurt her, but he didn't intend to release her until she talked to him.

Viva glared at him. "What exactly are you try-ing to prove, Spence? That you're physically stronger than I am, or that you can browbeat me into submission?"

He studied her through narrowed eyes. "You're as prickly as barbed wire. I don't get it."

"If you must know what's on my mind, it's the stack of work waiting for me at the office."

He shook his head. "Don't lie to me," he urged ever so softly, but there was steel in each and every word.

"There's no point in talking to you, is there? If I answer you, I'm lying. If I'm quiet, you're suspi-cious of my silence." She shook her head in frustra-tion, then settled back in her seat. "I warned you not to pressure me, Spence. Don't do it again, or you won't like the end result."

He released her hands. "Viva, I . . . ," he be-gan, but he fell silent as the announcer's voice boomed out of the loudspeaker.

Although they sat side by side, Spence realized that they were worlds apart. The realization ate at him, and he barely noticed the final race of opening day at Del Mar. He became preoccupied with the *why* of Viva's defensive attitude.

Spence remained subdued following the race

and during their encounter with friends at the Turf Club afterward. He thought Viva seemed more relaxed as he watched her circulate among the other owners gathered there.

Although he kept his feelings in check, he resented the men who persisted in waylaying her, regardless of their motives, just as he resented her smiles for them. He felt like an idiot, but he breathed a sigh of relief when she paused to join a couple who had enjoyed a lifelong friendship with her late uncle.

The sound of her voice as the three reminisced warmed him, and he couldn't help thinking, yet again, how much he'd depended on the easy camaraderie they'd shared in the past. He'd missed her on a variety of levels, and her abrupt disappearance had made him realize just how important their friendship had been to him.

His daughter, Emily, had counted on her too. Thanks to Viva she was now a college sophomore, which was nothing short of a miracle, since Emily had gotten mixed up in a rough high school crowd.

Viva had stepped into the middle of what had become a volatile father-daughter relationship. She'd counseled Emily, comforting the motherless girl as only another woman who had lost her own mother at a young age could before guiding her down a path that had led Em back to her academic pursuits.

"I have to be on my way," he heard Viva say.

As she retrieved her purse and stood, Spence

also pushed to his feet. "I'll walk you out," he offered.

"There's really no need. I—"

He cut in, "I want to bring you up to speed on Ben's schedule for working some of our horses."

Her smile faltered. She nodded, leaned down to hug Miriam and Stanley Houghton, and then promised, at Miriam's insistence, to attend their annual race-season dinner party the next weekend.

Spence followed Viva through the crowded restaurant. Along the way he acknowledged several friends and acquaintances with either a brusque nod or a monosyllabic greeting. Viva's haste to leave the racetrack blunted his usual affability.

"How's Emily?" she asked as they walked out of the Turf Club and began their stroll down the cavernous hallway that led to the stairs.

Spence cast a startled glance at her. "I was just thinking about her while you were talking to Miriam and Stan."

"And?"

"She's doing great. She loves school so much that she stayed on campus this summer to take a couple of extra science classes."

Viva smiled. "She should be about ready to declare her major course of study. Does she still want to go into veterinary medicine?"

"That's what she says. And once she sets her mind on something, I've discovered that it's hazardous to try and persuade her otherwise."

"Stubborn to the end. Just like someone else I

know," Viva teased, her footsteps slowing as they approached one of several steep staircases situated throughout the multistoried grandstand complex.

Responding to her lightened mood, he chuckled. "I like to think of it as having a strong character."

She laughed. "I'm sure you do."

Spence paused on the landing in front of the wide cement staircase, aware that it was the first time he'd heard that particular sound in a very long time, aware, too, of how much he'd missed it.

Viva's encompassing smiles and easy laughter had always been essential to her nature, but she'd misplaced her laughter, and her smiles seemed rare. Spence wanted both attributes restored, and he promised himself that he would do everything in his power to make certain that they were.

"Did I ever say a proper thank-you for everything you did for her?" he asked.

Viva smiled. "I love her, Spence. Thanks aren't necessary."

"You turned her around."

Viva shook her head. "Emily turned herself around," she corrected gently. "She knew she was in trouble, and she decided to do something about it. All I did was reassure her that her situation was salvageable, and that she owed herself a second chance."

"You still deserve some of the applause. I might have lost her if it hadn't been for you."

"You didn't lose her, though, and I doubt you would have. She is, after all, her father's daughter."

This is how it used to be between us, Spence thought as he searched her features.

Viva looked away almost immediately. Spence felt certain then that she realized what he was thinking, and he couldn't help wondering if she felt the same way. He hoped so.

"She's been worried about you, even though she defended you for leaving," he said in reference to the events of fourteen months earlier. "When I spoke to her this morning, she said to tell you that she wants to see you."

Viva nodded, the animation departing her heart-shaped face. "Please give her my love when you talk to her next." She glanced at her watch. "I have to leave." Moving past Spence, she started down the stairs with as much haste as her high-heeled pumps would allow.

Frustrated anew with Viva, he followed her. He felt rather than saw her lose her balance near the bottom of the stairs. Spence grabbed her arm and steadied her before she tumbled forward.

The wide-brimmed hat she wore went flying as she jerked her head up. An alarmed sound escaped her. Twisting against his hold, she tried to wrench free of him.

Spence swept her off her feet and carried her the remainder of the way down the stairs. He placed his hands on her shoulders once she was standing in front of him. "What's wrong with you?

I was just trying to keep you from taking a header when you lost your footing."

"Let go of me," she insisted, growing more pale with every passing second.

When he didn't respond to her order, Viva muttered an angry word and renewed her attempt to free herself. Spence tightened his hold on her. Her long, straight hair tumbled free of the loose topknot she'd fashioned earlier in the day as she tried to escape him. He watched it cascade across her shoulders like an unraveling bolt of dark chocolate satin. Gripping her upper arms, he gave her a hard shake when she continued to struggle.

"Damn you!" she seethed, but only loud enough for him to hear the words as two men passed them on the landing.

He responded to the woman and her anger in a way that startled even him. Life had taught him never to react to anything or anyone impulsively, but he found it impossible not to draw Viva into his arms and claim what he wanted.

The last thing Spence saw was the shock in her huge eyes before they fluttered closed. The last coherent thought he had was that he needed a taste of her—just one taste of the sensuality that lurked beneath the surface of this woman who was usually so composed. She was no more composed than a storm-tossed sea. But then, neither was he.

She pulled back slightly when his lips first settled against hers. He paused, wondering if he'd lost his mind. His gut told him he probably had, but he didn't care any longer. The rules between them had changed fourteen months earlier, and there was no going back.

Clearly stunned by his actions, Viva went as still as stone, but her resistance to Spence's touch ended on the heels of a raggedly indrawn breath. He heard her whisper his name a few seconds later. He heard shock and confusion, but nothing even vaguely resembling a protest.

Relieved, he angled his head, his lips gentle as he molded them to hers. He felt the trembling of her body and knew it reflected the stunning desire resonating within his own.

Viva didn't pull away this time. Neither did Spence. He knew he couldn't, so he didn't waste the time required to summon the effort.

He slowly tested the resilience of her lips, then sucked at her lower one. He teethed it with great care and at his leisure. He didn't care that they were in a public place. He didn't care about anything but Viva and the desire streaking into his bloodstream like a fiery comet.

The shaky sigh that slipped past her lips fueled his desire for her. After inhaling the sound, he traced the seam of her lips with the tip of his tongue. He shuddered when she began to part her lips and accepted the invitation implicit in her tentative gesture.

Delving directly into the heat of her, he discovered that she tasted as sweet as a succulent peach picked at the peak of the season. It was a flavor he knew he would forever connect to Viva, in the same way that he connected the faint scent of vanilla and exotic spices to her skin.

Voices sounded a few seconds later. The clatter of footsteps on cement followed, reminding Spence of how exposed they were. Unwilling to subject Viva to the prying eyes of strangers, he lifted his head, spied a shallow alcove a few feet away, and guided her to it.

"We can't . . . ," she began, her voice a breathless whisper that heightened his hunger for another sample of her.

"We are," he said rawly.

He framed her features with his broad-palmed hands, hands that shook when he saw the expression on her face—an expression that reflected equal parts disbelief, shock, and fear. It was her fear that gut-punched him. He felt compelled to dispel it. Later, he promised himself, he would discover the reason for it, but for now he simply wanted it gone.

Reclaiming her mouth, he gathered her against his hard frame, allowing her to feel the desire throbbing in his loins even as he savored the way in which she fit against his body. A perfect fit. The lushness of her figure, her full breasts plumped against his chest, and her hips curved enticingly against the hardness of his loins and thighs, aroused him even more. He deepened their kiss, but this time without the restraint he'd employed the first time.

He wanted her too much. He took what he

needed and he gave in return, his hands smoothing up and down her back, pausing to span the nothingness of her waist, and then cupping her hips and urging her closer.

With his senses fully engaged, he drank in the essence of her, his tongue sweeping over the interior surfaces of her mouth with a thoroughness that had them both gasping for breath almost instantly.

It was insanity and fate combined, he concluded before lucid thought fled and he surrendered to the moment.

She answered his passion with her own. She came alive in his embrace, her response as stunning to him as a sudden flash of heat lightning zigzagging across a Kentucky night sky.

She tangled her tongue with his, then nipped at the tip before sucking it deeply into her mouth. Spence shuddered again, the need for more of her clamoring within him. He knew then that she would be a volatile lover.

His touch grew acutely possessive, instinct driving him with a relentlessness that felt vaguely foreign to him, but he didn't resist. Known for his control and sense of propriety, he felt totally without control as his desire for Viva reigned supreme.

Bracketing her hips with his hands, he shifted against her pelvis, the ache in his loins so profound that he wanted nothing more than to bury himself as deeply as possible within her.

Moaning softly into his mouth, the sound a blending of intense desire and frustration, Viva dug her fingers into his lower back, kneading like a feline who hungered for fruition as she clung to him. She unknowingly provoked images in his mind of what it would be like to have her in his bed. She seduced him in a thousand little ways.

Spence felt the violent tremor that ripped through her. His own body near flash point, he forced himself to stop, forced himself to free her lips, although he kept his arms around her. As he held her, he listened to her gasp for breath. Despite the agony holding himself in check caused, he didn't release her until they both stopped shaking.

"Are you seeing anyone?" he asked once words were possible.

She raised startled eyes to his face.

When she didn't answer, he put a few more inches of space between them. "I won't share you."

Viva paled. "Spence, this can't happen again."

"It will happen."

She shook her head. "No," she insisted. "It cannot and will not happen again. Why don't we just chalk it up to a moment of insanity and forget it? You're angry with me, and in the heat of the moment we—"

"No! This isn't about anger." He kept his gaze on her features as he took one of her hands and pressed it against his loins. "This is about arousal."

She jerked her hand away. "You're being deliberately crude."

"I'm being honest. Try it, Viva. I've discovered

that it makes life a whole lot simpler over the long haul."

Anger sharpened her voice. "I won't be one of your conquests, Spence."

He frowned. "That's not my style, and you know it."

"You're right," she conceded softly. "It's not your style, but this conversation is still pointless." She turned away from him.

He caught her by placing his hand on her shoulder. She glanced at him, and he saw the tears glistening in her eyes. "I don't understand what's happening between us any more than you do, but I'll be damned if I'll dismiss it as inconsequential," he admitted.

"Let it go, for both our sakes," she urged.

"I can't." As the words left his mouth, he knew he spoke the truth. This wasn't a simple matter of a man who wanted to seduce a desirable woman into his bed. There was much more at stake, he realized, even if he couldn't yet define it. "Viva, I can't let go."

"You don't have any other choice," she whispered.

Unwilling to argue with her, Spence rescued her wide-brimmed hat from the floor and handed it to her without saying a word.

"Thank you." She walked away then, and she didn't look back.

Spence didn't try to stop her.

THREE

Viva braced herself for her meeting with Spence and the trainer who handled all of the partnership horses. She briefly considered canceling, but in the end she decided that delaying tactics on her part would heighten Spence's interest, not mute it.

She wanted him so much now that she'd begun to feel obsessed by her desire for him. During the preceding two days thoughts of him had invaded her dreams and ruined her concentration at the office. Even her secretary had commented on how preoccupied she seemed.

Viva finally concluded that behaving as though nothing significant had occurred between them would be her wisest course of action. She would simply have to conceal the shock and desire that continued to reverberate within her in the aftermath of the passionate exchange they'd shared.

Because of Spence, she felt more in tune with

herself as a woman than she'd ever felt in her entire thirty-four years, despite the frustration inherent in desiring a man her common sense insisted she couldn't have.

Clad in jeans, T-shirt, and boots, Viva arrived shortly after dawn at the entrance to the stable area of the Del Mar racetrack. She recalled the general layout of the stables and backstretch portion of the track from previous trips in past years with Uncle Tommy.

She stopped at the security gate. The guard stationed there provided her with a guest pass. After guiding her car along the rutted road that wound through the sprawling stable complex, she parked in a makeshift dirt lot.

Thanks to the message Spence had left on her voice mail, Viva easily located Ben Wilding, a British-born, third-generation horse trainer who possessed the kind of respect in the Thoroughbred community normally reserved for men and women many years his senior.

She paused in the doorway of his office. "Hello, Ben. It's good to see you again."

He got up from his desk and approached her. "Miss Conrad, it's been a long time. You're looking well." The epitome of his conversative roots, Ben shook her hand and offered a restrained smile.

"How long have we known each other, Ben?"

"Seven years, Miss Conrad."

"Then I think it's past time for you to call me Viva. Miss Conrad was my great-aunt, and she's been a permanent resident of Mount Hope Cemetery since before I was born."

The lanky thirty-two-year-old gave her a startled look.

Viva grinned. "I'm not letting you off the hook, Ben. I won't answer to anything but my first name, so consider yourself warned."

He nodded, a hint of an answering smile visible in his lean facial features. "I'll try," he promised. "Would you like a tour of the stables while we wait for Mr. Hammond?"

"He isn't here yet?"

"He's running late this morning."

A reprieve, she thought, her spirits lifting, although she kept her relief to herself. "That's too bad," she remarked as they walked outside. She glanced around, taking in the early morning activity typical in racetrack stables across the world. "I haven't been here in a few years, but things don't appear to have changed all that much."

"No, they haven't." Ben hesitated, then said, "I hope you'll accept my condolences. Mr. Conrad will be missed by a lot of people, especially me. He and Mr. Hammond were the first owners to employ me here in America when I decided to go out on my own."

As the two talked, they crossed the breezeway that separated the office from the adjacent stable.

"Uncle Tommy believed in creating opportunities for talented people. He trusted and admired you, but I don't think I'm telling you something you haven't already figured out for yourself."

"I'll always remember him as a generous man."

As they threaded their way through the workers caring for the horses, they paused in front of a series of stalls. Ben supplied the name and breeding history of each Thoroughbred, as well as the identity of the owner. Viva knew some personally, others by reputation.

Hired simultaneously by more than a dozen owners, Ben and his employees were responsible for more than forty horses during the Del Mar meet alone. Viva privately marveled at his ability to juggle the needs of the animals, not to mention the varietal personalities of the owners.

She also understood the added challenge to Ben when the horses he trained were in competition on the track. His integrity and judicious handling of awkward situations, she knew, invariably eliminated any question of bias.

As Ben provided a description of the workout schedule for the partnership horses, she heard herself asking the kinds of questions often voiced by her uncle. Their conversation served to remind her that her Kentucky roots ran deep—too deep to abandon indefinitely.

She'd lived and breathed Thoroughbred horse racing since birth, first with her parents on their breeding farm, then with Uncle Tommy at Oakbrook Farm. The ease with which she slipped into her role of owner didn't escape her. Viva discovered that it hadn't escaped Spence's attention either, when she glanced over her shoulder and spotted him standing just a few feet away.

Her insides quivered. Ben's voice faded to a soft hum as she met Spence's gaze. In that brief, unguarded moment Viva felt both transparent and vulnerable.

Lifting her chin, she exerted the kind of self-control that she'd learned to employ in recent years. A heartbeat later she noticed the smile that tugged at the corners of Spence's mouth as he peered back at her.

Viva recognized that smile, and it put a dent in her facade of indifference. It was the smile that made him look vaguely boyish at forty-two, but it was also the same smile that had the power to make a smart woman stupid. She'd seen a sufficient number of examples of that particular malady over the years to be cautious now.

She kept her expression even. She also kept her distance and her emotions in check, and was relieved when his smile finally faded. She glanced reassuringly at Ben when she noticed his curious expression.

"Morning, Ben," Spence said, filling the silence Viva had created.

"Mr. Hammond." The trainer stepped forward to shake hands with his client. "It's good to see you again, sir."

Viva offered Spence a cool nod of acknowledgment, then shifted her attention to the filly being groomed in the bathing area between two of the six stables assigned to Ben.

"I spoke to the vet about Night Wing this morning," he commented to the trainer. "She seems optimistic that he'll be able to race in another three to four weeks."

Ben nodded. "I agree. His tendon injury is healing nicely, so I thought I'd work him slowly back up to the times we achieved at Hollywood Park. His breezes were excellent while he was there."

As the two men discussed Night Wing, Viva reflected on the similarities between Olympic-level athletes and the finest Thoroughbreds. Both trained for endurance and speed. Despite the impressive size and strength of the horses, however, they could be as fragile as the finest crystal and as fractious as any two-year-old child. And, like the latter, just as dependent on patience, consistency, and affection.

"You're enjoying yourself, aren't you?"

Viva shrugged out from under the arm that Spence had slipped around her shoulders. Turning, she faced him. "Of course I'm enjoying myself. You needn't sound so surprised."

"You turned your back on your life. What else was I supposed to think?"

"Sometimes the truth is less than obvious, Spence."

He scowled at her. "There was a time when I understood you."

"Times change. So do people."

"The real question is why?"

Stay calm, she counseled herself, even though she wanted nothing more than to submerge herself in his sensuality and forget her worry about his well-being. She couldn't do either of those things, though. "I'm not inclined to spar with you this morning, Spence."

He took her arm as they walked past several stalls. "What are you inclined to do these days?" he asked, his voice low and his gaze probing as he scanned her face.

Viva ignored the innuendo in his tone, freed her arm, and glanced at her watch. "I'm inclined to be on my way, since you and Ben don't really need me."

"Why do you pull away every time I touch you?"

"Why do you insist on touching me?" she countered.

"You didn't mind it two days ago."

"That was then, and this is now."

"You wanted me."

"I've wanted things before that weren't right for me."

"I'm not a thing, Viva," he reminded her.

"I thought you were a friend."

"You know I am."

She pressed her fingertips to her temple, then took a steadying breath. "I don't know anything any longer."

"Mr. Hammond . . ."

Glad that Ben had interrupted them, Viva flashed a quick smile at the trainer. "Thanks for the tour, Ben. I'll see you soon."

Viva immediately began the short trek back to her car. She reached the vehicle before she realized that Spence had followed her, but she didn't look at him until she'd unlocked her door and pulled it open.

"You're going to run forever, aren't you?"

She tossed her purse onto the seat before she answered him. "I need to get to the office for a meeting."

"And I need you, Viva." He spoke softly. "So where do we go from here?"

The underlying intensity in his voice conveyed a depth of hunger that shook Viva's composure. She realized that it matched her own. "Nowhere, Spence. We go nowhere. You don't need me. You want me. There's a difference, and we both know it."

"Need. Want. This isn't the time for a game of semantics." He shrugged, but the casual gesture was at odds with his rigid posture. "The words mean the same thing in the end."

"Needing and wanting aren't issues I'm willing to explore with you. We're business partners, courtesy of Uncle Tommy. What happened the other day was an error in judgment that I don't plan to repeat."

"I think you want me. I also think you need me as much as I need you."

You have no idea just how much, she thought. "Think whatever you like, since you always do, but I'm leaving. I'm behind schedule, and the morning freeway traffic is awful."

He reached for her, his hands curving over her shoulders. He held her in place, making her aware of the leashed power contained in his lean, muscled frame, aware as well of how susceptible she was to him.

Viva shifted uneasily beneath his hands. She tried to move beyond him, but she was trapped between her car and his body.

"Stop acting like I'm going to attack you," he ordered.

Anger and frustration burst to life inside her. She glared at him. "Then quit stalking me. I've made my position clear. All I'm interested in is our business relationship. Nothing else."

Although he looked stunned, he recovered quickly. "You're overreacting. And for the record, I've never stalked a woman in my life, and I sure as hell don't plan on starting now."

"I shouldn't have said that," she conceded, softening her stance because she knew he was right.

She felt some of the tension her thoughtless remark had caused drain out of him. She also felt the changes taking place in her own body as the warmth of his palms and fingers seeped through the cotton of her shirt.

She bit back the plea for intimacy hovering on the tip of her tongue. She didn't know what to do or say when she noticed the desire that flared to life in Spence's gaze.

They stared at each other for several moments. The emotions and sensations flowing through her heart and body weakened Viva's knees. She brought her hands to Spence's narrow waist, only vaguely aware that she was using his sturdy body to steady herself.

He smoothed his fingertips up and down her arms, his voice roughly seductive as he said, "I'm not kidding around either. I've never been more serious about anything in my entire life."

Viva shivered. She didn't resist when he gathered her into his arms. He drew her into his heat and hardness with a gentleness that made her tremble.

With tears stinging her eyes, she made herself endure the temptation posed by his body and the alluring scent of his aftershave. This was the kind of intimacy that she'd dreamed of and prayed for with Spence Hammond.

In a perfect world she would have accepted what he offered and enjoyed the luxury of transforming a dream into reality. She would have welcomed his desire, the sense of being valued, and his willingness to share his strength with those he cared about. In a perfect world he would have wanted everything she longed to give. He would have wanted all of her. Especially her love.

But she'd relearned a bitter lesson in the last fourteen months, the same lesson she'd learned as a child on the day that her parents had died. The world was an imperfect place, and their current circumstances had them all teetering on the brink of disaster, even if Spence didn't know it.

Viva remembered then what a mistake in judgment on her part might yield. She shuddered, resisting the memory of finding Michael after his murder, but the image filled her mind and refused to depart. The thought of Spence and Emily suffering a similar fate terrified her.

"You're safe, little one."

Shocked, she stared at him.

He frowned at her reaction. "What's got you so frightened?"

She searched his features and saw only confusion. "Nothing."

"I don't believe you." He whispered the words, his voice resembling a caress.

Revealing the truth was so tempting, if only to end her fear and isolation, but Viva knew that Spence would feel compelled to confront the person who'd ordered Michael's death. She might lose him forever. The injustice of their predicament hit her like a blow from a closed fist. Some of the barriers she'd constructed around her emotions started to crumble.

Suddenly too weak to resist the combined impact of her own need and his nearness, Viva sank against Spence, accepting his strength and savoring his closeness. She gave herself permission to steal a few crumbs of happiness, but only for a brief time.

When her conscience warned her about impulsive behavior, she rationalized her actions with the reasoning that a couple of minutes in Spence's embrace would help to sustain her in the weeks and months, maybe even years, ahead. She needed him, now more than ever.

"I've missed you," he murmured against her temple as he held her. "More than I realized until I showed up at your office the other night and saw you again."

Viva tried to speak, but the emotions simmering inside her turned into a roiling cauldron and threatened to overwhelm her. She nodded in response to his remark, then tucked her face into the muscular curve that joined his neck and shoulder.

She stood there trembling, clinging to him, and so desperately hungry for him that she wanted to surrender to the desire spinning recklessly through her heart and body. She felt exposed, naked all the way to her soul, and more vulnerable than at any time in her entire life.

Alarmed by her dwindling control, Viva fought for inner balance. She found it, but her victory proved to be short-lived.

Drawing back, Spence tunneled his fingers into her thick hair, dislodging the loose braid she'd fashioned earlier and freeing the dense dark mass so that it flowed over her shoulders and down her back. As he framed her face between his palms, she stared up at him, blue eyes wide and lips slightly parted as she tried to control her erratic breathing.

He muttered a word that might have sounded coarse under any other conditions, but it echoed in her ears with a curious kind of reverence. Spence lowered his head, blocking out the morning sun and thwarting any protest she might have managed as his lips settled over hers.

Viva moaned, but not to object. Never to object. Relief permeated the inarticulate sound. Utter relief.

Spence drank in her surrender with the next breath he took. Angling his head, he kissed her with a thoroughness that made her head spin.

She brought her hands to his shoulders and gripped the wide expanse. Her breasts flattened against his chest and her pelvis mated with his loins as she molded herself to him. She felt the answering surge of male flesh and tried to get even closer to him.

As he plunged his tongue into her mouth and bracketed her hips between his hands, she knew she'd never before been the focus of such intense desire. She'd never been kissed as though she was essential to the survival of a man. And she'd never felt more combustible or alive. She felt all those things now, and others, as Spence plundered her mouth like a man starved for the sustenance that only she could provide.

The sheer lushness of the sensations whirling around inside her eclipsed her anxiety and banished whatever resistance she might have summoned. She twisted against Spence, shifting back and forth until her body vibrated with unappeased hunger. She skimmed her hands across his shoulders before she tangled her fingers at his nape, and her mouth grew as avid as his.

He wrenched free of her without warning a few minutes later. Senses reeling, Viva sagged in his embrace. Shaking from head to toes, she tried to catch her breath.

"Come with me to my suite at L'Auberge," he urged before he claimed her mouth again.

She wanted nothing more than to accept his invitation, but she didn't dare. Something deep inside of her—hope, she later decided—shattered into a thousand pieces. The despair she felt almost drove her to her knees. She was behaving like a fool, and she knew it. Just as she knew that accompanying Spence to his hotel would simply compound the poor judgment of the last several minutes.

She ducked her head, feeling the loss of his lips instantly. "Stop, please," she said, trying to extricate herself from his embrace. "Don't do this to me."

His disbelief showed in his taut facial features. "Why not? It's what we both want."

She shook her head. "Wanting isn't enough."

"It's a place to start, Viva."

"We've started something we can't finish."

"Tell me why," he demanded.

"Let me go."

He released her, but his tension remained evident. "You owe me an explanation."

Giving him a belligerent look, she announced, "I don't have one to offer."

"Then explain this insane self-exile you've undertaken."

True to his nature, he'd shifted mental gears with a dexterity that brought Viva up short. "You're pressuring me again," she cautioned.

"Is that why you're shaking like a palsy victim."

Viva said the first thing that came to mind. "I always react this way when I feel cornered."

"Cornered?" He sounded incredulous.

Viva hardly blamed him. "I didn't mean physically. I invited what just happened between us."

"Then what the hell did you mean?"

"Emotionally. I'm not sure what the future holds for me, Spence. I can't make choices like the one you're asking me to make, at least not now."

He suddenly paled, and worry filled his dark eyes. "Are you ill? Is that why you left?"

Just sick at heart, she thought. "My health is fine, but I need you to stop trying to manipulate me. Please, for both our sakes."

"Why?" he insisted, his voice raised. "Tell me why you left Kentucky, dammit!"

She shoved at him with both hands, her patience and self-control disintegrating in the face of his anger. "Don't shout at me."

Spence calmed himself with obvious effort. "Viva, this is nuts. Your emotions are all over the map every time we get together. I think we need to talk once we've both cooled off."

She exhaled in a gust. "Think what you like. I'm not coming back to the track, Spence. Don't call me, and don't show up at my office. Forget my name. Forget me." As soon as the words left her mouth, she wanted to retrieve them. The last thing she wanted was his continued absence from her life. It broke her heart to imagine her days and nights without him.

Viva saw his stricken expression, and it prompted her realization that the only way to protect him was to alienate him. As much as she hated doing it, she knew she had no choice.

One of the things she loved most about Spence was his persistent, never-say-die mentality when he pursued a goal, but it was a double-edged sword at the moment. They couldn't afford the penalties involved if he achieved his goal this time. She forced herself to speak. "I won't be managed into submission or mauled in order to satisfy any man's sexual needs."

"You've got to be kidding," he muttered. "What the hell's gotten into you?"

Instead of answering his question, Viva deliberately demanded, "Don't the rules for being a gentleman apply when we're together?"

"Dammit, Viva! You wanted me two days ago, and you wanted me two minutes ago. Those are indisputable facts."

"I'm not interested, and that is a fact that you'd better take seriously."

He seized her wrist and placed his fingertips over the pulse throbbing there. "It's racing."

She jerked free of his grip. "I'm angry."

"You might be angry, but you're also as turned on as a thousand-watt lightbulb."

End this now, an inner voice counseled. "Good-bye, Spence." She slipped into the passenger seat of her car and reached for the seat belt.

He didn't attempt to stop her, although he grabbed the door before she could shut it. Leaning down, he pinned her with a hard look. "You're kidding yourself if you think I'm going to forget you or leave you alone, Viva. I've just appointed myself your conscience, and I won't be silenced or ignored. I can live without sex with you, but I won't rest until I have the truth. The whole truth."

Straightening, he shoved the car door closed with such force that it slammed and shook the vehicle like an exclamation mark at the end of an epithet.

Viva managed to start her car and drive away, but with considerable effort. When she glanced in her rearview mirror, she saw Spence standing where she'd left him. She realized then that her plan had backfired. Instead of alienating him, she'd aroused his curiosity even more.

FOUR

The telephone call came later that same night. Jarred out of a fitful sleep, Viva immediately recognized the voice of the caller. The distinctive sound sent a chill across her soul and catapulted her back in time to the day of Michael's funeral.

"You've been seen at the racetrack by mutual acquaintances."

His observation didn't surprise her. She'd long suspected that he had people watching her. "I had no choice." Viva spoke the truth, but she wondered if he believed her.

"We always have choices, Miss Conrad."

You haven't given me any, she thought angrily. "I gather you're aware of my uncle's recent death."

"Of course."

"And of the terms of his will?"

"It is, after all, a matter of public record."

"Then you must realize . . . ," she began.

"What I realize is that you are in violation of our contract," he said with the sharpness of a finely honed blade. "How do you propose to resolve the situation?"

Her heart raced as panic started to riddle her composure, but she refused to give him the satisfaction of sounding like a frightened child. "I am attempting to extricate myself, both personally and legally, from an active role in all matters concerning Oakbrook Farm, but without arousing the suspicions of those involved."

"Ah, Mr. Hammond is being difficult. I can always deal with him for you."

Dear God! "That won't be necessary. He knows nothing about our . . . arrangement."

"Which is why Hammond and his daughter are still alive," he reminded her.

Viva shivered despite the warmth of the balmy July night. "I know," she whispered.

"I am not happy, and there are consequences when my displeasure is prolonged."

She grasped all too well the deadly reach of this man. "I'm walking a very fine line in an effort to protect your privacy and meet your expectations," she said, verbally tiptoeing through a conversation that reminded her of a minefield. "In fact, I've told Spence that I'm willing to give him full power of attorney over my half of the partnership."

"And Mr. Hammond's response to your generosity?" he inquired.

She knew she couldn't tell him the truth. "He's considering my offer."

"He is reluctant to take advantage of your grief over your late uncle, I assume. A man of exceedingly high moral standards, our Mr. Hammond."

Unlike you, Viva thought bitterly. "Yes, he is."

"And he, of course, wouldn't want you to act in haste. He would also question the reasons for your desire to give up control over the most valuable portion of your inheritance."

"He was surprised," she conceded.

"He won't accept your offer," the caller predicted. "Which means I still may have to intercede on your behalf."

You malevolent son of the devil! "He hasn't given me a decision yet."

"He won't accept," he said tersely. "What other alternatives are you exploring?"

"I've asked my attorney for guidance with respect to creating a trust."

The caller chuckled.

Viva cringed, but she held on to her wits and her nerve as best as she could.

"Perhaps you should also consider relocating."

"My departure would arouse too much curiosity at this time," she commented. "I'd also need to train my replacement at the clinic, and that would take several weeks."

As she spoke, Viva couldn't quite believe how matter-of-fact she sounded. At the moment she wanted nothing more than a safe hiding place, but she doubted that one existed as long as this amoral creature occupied even a centimeter of space on the planet.

"Minor details," he said dismissively. "You could always sign over your interest in the partnership to me."

Not in a New York minute, Viva thought, because I will not permit you to put your greedy hands on everything Spence and Uncle Tommy worked so hard to create.

"You were very clear about not wanting to draw attention to yourself, and a move like that would be the equivalent of putting you under a spotlight," Viva pointed out, then held her breath because she feared she might have been too bold.

"Your concern for me is deeply gratifying, Miss Conrad. Ever the do-gooder, aren't you? What a shame, and a decided waste of your obvious charms. You're a beautiful woman . . . and under other circumstances . . ." He let the thought dangle.

Stunned, Viva fought the rush of nausea his comment spawned.

"Ah, well, fate is a fickle mistress at times, isn't she?"

"I promised you that I wouldn't . . ." Viva nearly choked on the word, but she made herself say it, ". . . compromise you. I haven't broken that promise, and I don't plan to. Too much is at stake."

"An honorable woman. You are indeed a rarity, Miss Conrad. In fact—"

"Then you won't . . ." Murder anyone else, she almost said, but she caught herself in time.

"You've interrupted me," he chided.

She held her breath.

"Aside from your notable physical charms, I've always admired your good manners and sense of decorum."

"Thank you." She waited several seconds before asking, "Will you give me the time I require in order to deal with my current situation?"

Silence.

Viva waited, although she longed to let out a scream of total frustration.

He exhaled, the sound rife with impatience. "See that you persuade Mr. Hammond to accept your offer. Use any means at your disposal, including seduction. In short, do whatever it takes, Miss Conrad."

Damn you to hell! Viva almost shouted. Instead, she simply said, "I understand."

"For the sake of all concerned, I certainly hope so. We'll speak again soon." He abruptly severed the connection.

In a state of shock, Viva gripped the phone and listened to the dial tone for several moments. She eventually shook herself free of the paralysis that had seized her.

After recradling the receiver, she covered her face with her hands and tried to calm herself enough for clear thought. She still found it hard to come to terms with the reality that she was under the proverbial thumb of a murderer and a racketeer.

Some people—she included herself on the list—also believed that he was responsible for the deaths of several valuable Thoroughbreds courtesy of insurance scams he'd allegedly masterminded. Viva privately considered him the kind of man capable of selling his own mother for the right sum of money. The fact that he'd suggested that she use her body to persuade Spence of anything classified him as a conscienceless bastard and added pimping to his list of crimes.

She sank back against the pillows, profoundly shaken by the bizarre telephone conversation. Viva stared into the darkness and considered her limited options.

She discarded the notion of leaving San Diego. She refused to flee into the night like a thief when she'd done nothing wrong. She believed that an unexplained departure on her part would place Spence and Emily in greater jeopardy, because Spence would come after her. Remaining in the area also allowed her to act as a buffer, albeit an unsubstantial one, between Spence and Emily and the threat against their lives.

As for her inheritance, she cared little about the money involved, but she planned to protect Tommy Conrad's legacy. The very thought of surrendering the empire he'd built to a criminal made her physically ill. She knew she owed Uncle Tommy more than she could ever repay, but in this instance she didn't intend to fail him.

Viva abandoned her bed a short while later. While she desperately needed a good night's sleep, her whirling thoughts made the endeavor impossible. She slipped into a light cotton robe and walked downstairs to the kitchen.

After filling a kettle with water and placing it on the stovetop to heat, she stood at the wall of windows that provided a panoramic view of the bay during the day. Lights from the navy aircraft carriers berthed at North Island twinkled in the darkness, as did the lights atop the skyscrapers that made up the downtown San Diego skyline.

She'd lived at the walled-in estate, now a portion of her inheritance, which was situated high on a hilltop in Point Loma, since arriving in southern California fourteen months earlier. Until now, it had felt like a safe haven. But not any longer. The wrong person knew her location, not just the unlisted phone number Uncle Tommy had arranged for her.

She shook her head, frustrated and unnerved by events over which she possessed little or no control. Viva couldn't remember a time, aside from the initial months following her departure from Kentucky, when she'd felt more alone or frightened.

The kettle began to whistle. Brushing aside the tears on her cheeks, she walked to the stove, turned off the flame beneath the kettle, and poured hot water over the tea bag in the mug she'd left on the nearby countertop. She glanced at the clock above the sink and noted the time—3:00 A.M. She cupped the mug between her palms while the tea steeped and scented the air with jasmine and orange.

The tea's fragrance reminded Viva of her mother, the woman who'd taught her, more by example than by design, that love, even if freely given, often required sacrifice. She knew, thanks to Tommy, that her mother had sacrificed her relationship with her parents, who'd considered her choice in a husband unsuitable for someone of her social background, when she'd married. Tommy had supported her decision, though, and he'd been there for his niece after the accident that had taken her parents. Where Spence was concerned, Viva willingly made the sacrifice of allowing him to think ill of her in order to protect him.

After removing the tea bag from her mug, Viva sipped the hot liquid and paced the exterior deck that extended along the entire back side of the hill-top estate. She knew what her next step had to be as the dawn edged across the sky a few hours later.

The week that followed was brutal. Viva functioned in a state of fear, but she made herself focus on the things she could control—preparation for the mid-year staff meetings at the clinic and the completion of federal grant applications that would provide additional funding for the portion of the clinic devoted to treating, at no charge, pediatric cases from low-income families in the community.

She instructed her secretary to screen all of her calls, and she worked a series of fourteen-hour days that would have felled an elephant. She paced the house late into the nights, too restless and on edge to sleep. Viva also ignored the logic that insisted she fuel her body with something more than tea, the occasional piece of fresh fruit, and dry toast, but her stomach rebelled when she attempted anything else.

Spence's growing anger with her avoidance tactics was obvious in the messages he left on her voice mail at the office, but Viva mentally crossed her fingers and counted on his hectic schedule to hold him at bay. The two times he showed up at the medical clinic, she was safely ensconced in a conference room when he pushed past her secretary and inspected her empty office for himself. She let the medical clinic staff believe that he was a rebuffed suitor.

Viva spoke several times that week to Harlan Wainright, Uncle Tommy's Kentucky attorney. Despite her insistence that she wanted a trust created as quickly as possible, Harlan counseled patience. Viva understood the cause—it was necessary to settle Tommy's estate before she could legally assume control of the assets. Only then could Harlan create the trust that would force Spence to consult the trustee on partnership matters.

Time was her greatest adversary at the moment,

because she had none to spare, but the ponderous machine called the legal process demanded patience and restraint on her part. With every hour that passed, however, she lived in terror that she was contributing to Spence and Emily's jeopardy rather than forestalling it.

Viva finally gave in to her physical and emotional fatigue eight days following her conversation with the late-night caller. Staggering with exhaustion, she arrived home near midnight, stripped off her clothing, showered, and fell into bed. Just as she started to doze off, the door chime sounded.

She ignored it at first, but the person at the front door persisted. She belatedly realized that someone had made his or her way past the estate's front gate. Had she forgotten to activate the security system? she wondered as she grabbed her robe and stepped into her slippers.

Without turning on any interior lights, Viva made her way to the door, peered through the security peephole, and saw the one person she longed to see. The very person she couldn't afford to see. She knew he wouldn't leave, so she jerked open the front door and confronted him.

"How did you find me?" she demanded. "And how did you get past the front gate?"

Spence stared at her for a long moment, then muttered a foul word.

Viva flinched. Gripping the edge of the door, she met his gaze with a belligerent expression on her face. "I asked you two questions."

"Harlan. He's worried about you. He gave me your address and the code to access the gate."

"He shouldn't be, and he shouldn't have. I'm fine."

Spence strode past her. "Yeah, you really look fine."

His sarcasm slammed into her like a wrecking ball. She swayed, then steadied herself. "Please leave."

He whirled to face her. "Not on your life."

Viva knew she couldn't force him to go. "It's late, Spence, and I'm very tired."

"You look like you've been dragged backward through a knothole."

She nodded. No point in denying the obvious, so she didn't waste her breath. "Why are you here?"

He gave her a look of pure annoyance. "Do you really have to ask?"

"I'm asking," Viva responded quietly. Easing shut the heavy teak front door, she walked down the hallway to the living room. She paused in the center of the room. She faced Spence with as much dignity and inner strength as she could possibly muster, but she suspected that she was outmanned and outgunned. He clearly held the advantage, though, since he appeared to be his usual take-charge self and she resembled what Uncle Tommy often called a walking-around disaster area.

"Say whatever it is you feel compelled to say, and then please leave."

He inspected her from head to toe with a critical gaze. "I have a lot to say. Let's start with, when did you last have a decent meal?"

Viva self-consciously tightened the sash on her floor-length silk robe. "My dietary habits don't concern you. Next question."

"Viva, you look as if you've lost ten pounds in the last week."

"Nine," she corrected, her tone neutral.

"What's going on with you? Have you been sick?"

"I've been busy at the office."

He dumped his briefcase on the nearest chair, then approached her.

Viva warily backed up two steps, then a third.

He paused, his exasperation with her apparent. "There's more going on here than professional obligations."

"Is there?" she asked.

"Dammit, Viva!"

She winced, then pressed her fingertips to the pulse hammering in her temple. "Please don't shout at me."

Looking mollified, Spence lowered his voice. "All right, I won't shout, but start talking to me. Now. I'm not leaving until I know what's wrong with you."

"Fatigue." She said the word with great care. Squaring her shoulders, she stiffened her spine. "A simple case of fatigue. That's all, Spence."

"I don't believe you."

She shrugged, trying to convey an indifference to his opinion that she didn't actually feel. In truth, his concern reassured her that she hadn't completely destroyed their friendship. "Your choice, of course. Are you done now?"

"No, I'm not done. I have some documents for you to sign."

"Leave them. I'll deal with them in the morning."

"No, we need to go over them together."

"Then call my secretary for an appointment."

He stared at her, clearly astounded by her attitude.

Viva took advantage of his silence. "You appear to have run out of questions, so I assume you're ready to leave now." She moved forward, intent on showing him to the door.

He seized her arm as she tried to sidestep him.

"Please, don't," she said, sounding strangled as she peered up at him.

"You're scaring me, Viva."

She gave him a wan smile. "Nothing scares you. That's one of the things I like most about you. You're utterly fearless."

He gave her a curious look. "Maybe I've changed too."

She shook her head. "That'll never happen. Besides, I don't want you to change. I need you to be you." She sighed. "I'm fine, so stop worrying, okay?"

"You keep saying that, but have you looked in a mirror lately?"

"I'm avoiding them at the moment." She glanced down at her wrist, feeling curiously detached in spite of the warmth of his touch. "Please take your hand away, Spence." *I don't trust myself when you touch me*, she thought to herself.

"You're liable to fall over if I do."

"Spence, please . . ." She stopped speaking as emotion she couldn't control welled up inside her.

He swore. The sound of the angry word came at her in waves, as though from a great distance. She met his alarmed gaze, and all her defenses toppled like falling bowling pins. "I can't . . . you don't . . . I'm . . ."

He stopped waiting for her to complete the disjointed sentence. Sweeping her up into his arms, he carried her to the couch and carefully placed her atop the overstuffed cushions. He reached for a few pillows and shoved them behind her back.

Viva stared up at him, tears pooling in her eyes. Her heart ached with regret for what might have been.

"Don't move."

"I couldn't even if I wanted to," she admitted.

"Where's the cognac?"

Uncle Tommy's drink of choice, she recalled. "The bar in the library. Down the hall. It's the second door on the right."

"I'll be right back. Don't get up. I've already

lost one partner, and I'm not in the mood to lose another."

Viva nodded and sank against the mound of pillows as he strode out of the living room. Closing her eyes, she breathed shallowly.

Spence returned a few minutes later, carrying a half-filled snifter and a plate of crackers. Sitting down beside her, he gave her the snifter. "Drink some of this."

She took the snifter. The amber liquid sloshed in her shaky grasp. She gripped it more tightly and brought it to her lips. It burned all the way down to her empty stomach.

"What in hell are you trying to do to yourself? Join Tommy and Michael?"

She exhaled, pulled away from him, and started to get up.

Spence pulled her back down beside him. "I want an answer."

"I'm thirty-four, Spence, not fourteen. I don't need a keeper."

"You need a whole lot of things, starting with some common sense, or you're going to wind up in a hospital."

"This is a tough time of year at the office."

"Viva, do you actually think I'm that stupid? This isn't about work. This is personal. This is about Michael, Tommy, and the reason, as yet unknown, why you left home. You can't convince me otherwise, so quit trying, all right?"

"All right," she said agreeably.

He scowled at her, but he didn't bother to pursue the matter. "I didn't have time for supper, and I'm still pretty good in the kitchen. I noticed that you have all the ingredients for an omelet when I checked out your refrigerator. Why don't I fix one? We can share it. Like we used to do in the old days."

"Will you leave if I let you feed me?" she asked, taking the path of least resistance because she wanted a little time with him. And because she knew that he wanted to do something tangible for her. He was that kind of a man. That kind of a friend.

He got to his feet, extending his hand to her as he spoke. "No promises unless you clean your plate."

"I need my beauty sleep," she teased.

"Come on, little one," he urged, tugging her to her feet. "You need more than sleep, but we'll start with food."

She cautioned, "I'm holding you to our agreement."

"You can try." He took her hand and led her to the kitchen. "You're the peanut gallery for this operation, so grab a stool," he ordered.

She did as instructed, a half smile teasing her lips as she climbed atop the stool at the far end of the butcher-block island in the center of the kitchen and crossed her legs.

Spence's gaze dropped to her exposed limbs.

He grinned at her. "Nice sticks. I hope you have them well insured."

Flushing, she covered her legs and sat a little taller on the stool. "You've been hired to cook, not ogle the lady of the house."

He opened the refrigerator door and started extracting ingredients for one of his world-class omelets. "So sue me," he advised, sounding relaxed for the first time that night.

"I'm too busy."

He paused and studied her, his humor fading.

She stared back at him, holding her breath. She wondered what he was thinking.

"You never used to be too busy, Viva," he finally said.

She exhaled in a rush, then spoke despite the emotion swelling in her throat. "I know, and I wish things were different, Spence. I'd give anything if they were different."

FIVE

"That was wonderful," Viva told Spence as she set aside her fork and sank back in her chair nearly an hour later.

After surveying her empty plate, he flashed a smile of approval at her. "That must mean I haven't lost my touch with an omelet pan."

She laughed. "It means you've got an alternate profession as a chef if you ever decide to give up the entrepreneur business."

He placed his napkin on the table beside his plate. "Never happen."

Viva nodded, then reached for the carafe situated between them on the table. "More coffee?"

Watching her pour a half-cup refill for herself, Spence took pleasure in how much more relaxed Viva seemed now that she'd eaten. "Not if I want to get any sleep tonight. And speaking of sleep, it's time for you to get some. You almost nodded off halfway through your omelet and toast."

"Dishes first," she insisted.

He shook his head in amusement. "Your work ethic hasn't diminished, has it?"

She sobered. "Considering who raised me, I doubt it ever will."

Spence studied her for a few moments. He realized that Tommy's recent death had affected Viva more deeply than he'd originally thought. At first he hadn't been able to move past his anger over her absence from the older man's bedside during the final year of his life, but the preceding two weeks had persuaded him that Viva had had a deep emotional response to his passing.

As Viva met his speculative gaze and withstood his inspection without comment, Spence knew he'd been very hard on her since his arrival in San Diego. He now regretted his judgmental attitude. Her composure as she sat there didn't surprise him. He sensed a new depth in her character, the kind of depth that found its origins in being tested by the anguish of losses endured and survived.

He wondered then if she would ever feel able to share with him the more private of her emotions. He wanted to know what made her sad and what brought her joy. He wanted to know everything, he realized. He wanted to give, as well.

Spence abruptly shoved his chair back from the table and got to his feet. Gathering up his plate and silverware, he crossed the spacious kitchen and placed the items in the sink.

Viva followed suit, carrying the empty platter and butter dish. "Let's leave these to soak. I'll clean up in the morning."

"Makes sense to me." Spence watched her make a second trip to the table in the breakfast nook for a few odds and ends from their meal. "Why don't you go on to bed?"

"Soon," she promised. "I think I'm finally relaxed enough to sleep."

"You haven't been doing much of that lately, have you?" Spence didn't bother to conceal his concern.

"I've had a lot on my mind."

"Like what?" He really didn't expect her to itemize the reasons for her insomnia, but he asked the question nonetheless.

She glanced at him, then shrugged. "Just a lot of little stuff. Nothing for you to worry about. I should sleep like a rock tonight, though. Lord knows, I'm tired enough."

"Why drive yourself so hard, Viva? You've never really needed to, and now there's no need at all," he said, aware of the fortune she would soon control.

"Must be that devil work ethic," she quipped as she finished filling the sink with warm, soapy water. "It's ingrained in me."

Spence caught her arm when she started to step away from him. He hated it when she felt compelled to put any distance between them, but he withdrew his hand when she stiffened beneath his touch.

"Sorry. I'm more tired than I realized," she said as if in explanation for her reaction.

"Tommy wouldn't have wanted you to—"

"Uncle Tommy is gone, Spence," she broke in, "but when he was alive, he never interfered in the choices I made."

"Am I interfering, or am I pointing out the merit of some old-fashioned logic? How exactly do you propose to run a business like Oakbrook Farm and manage a medical clinic at the same time?"

"I'm still considering my options." Viva looked away as she spoke.

"Coming home probably makes the most sense."

"Only to a certain degree," she hedged.

He saw the tension in her features. "I don't want to argue with you, but we both know you're not going to be able to put off making some tough decisions in the very near future."

She sighed. "You aren't telling me something I haven't already figured out."

"Then stop holding me at arm's length, and let me help you," he urged.

"I don't need to be rescued, Spence, and I'm too old to be treated like a child. When I want help, I'll ask for it. Until then, I'll do my best with what is, admittedly, a difficult situation. Let's not spoil a lovely couple of hours and one of your world-class omelets with any more talk about decisions and responsibilities. It's late, and as you so aptly put it a little while ago, I look like I've been dragged backward through a knothole. You may have dented my ego, but there's no denying the obvious."

He nodded, frustrated with her unwillingness to confide in him, but smart enough to know that he couldn't force her to talk. "If you decide to open up or if you need a sounding board, I'm available. The choices you're about to make have a direct impact on my future, so I have a vested interest in whatever you do."

She trembled as she met his hard gaze. "I know, Spence. Believe me, I know."

When he saw the tears welling in her eyes before she turned away, he swore softly and reached for her. "Don't run away from me, Viva. I'm not trying to hurt or manipulate you."

Bowing her head, she pressed her fingertips to her temples. "I trust you, but I need to work this through on my own."

He very gently drew her back against his sturdy body and wrapped his arms around her. Leaning down, he pressed a kiss to the side of her face, then nuzzled her neck. Her unique fragrance filled his senses and evoked urges of a purely sensual nature.

Viva shuddered, but she didn't try to move away from him.

He felt her slowly start to relax, felt her settle against him as she rested the back of her head on his shoulder, felt and heard the heavy sigh that flowed out of her.

He longed to comfort her, but he satisfied his yearning with an unthreatening embrace. He suspected that she would reject anything she thought smacked of condescension or a rescue attempt or even seduction. He considered her innate pride a double-edged sword at the moment. He again resolved to offer her the strength of his friendship, but nothing more, because he didn't want her to feel pressured.

They stood there for several quiet minutes. The silence they shared was periodically punctuated by the faint moan of a distant foghorn. Otherwise, neither one spoke or moved.

Spence reflected on the level of desire Viva evoked within him. He knew he'd never experienced anything quite like it in his entire adult life, and he didn't completely understand his response to her. With other women, he'd always contained and controlled his biological urges with ease, but with Viva he struggled. Constantly.

If his desire for her hadn't been so soul-deep, he might have felt amused and written it off. But this was Viva, and she'd always occupied a special place in his life.

"I think it's time for you to go," she eventually said.

Spence disagreed. It was late, and he was reluctant to leave her alone. "Why don't I use one of the guest rooms?"

She turned slowly in the circle of his arms. She peered up at him, her expression troubled.

His body reacted to the brush of her breasts against his chest and the perfect alignment of her hips to his loins. He tried to conceal his response, but he failed. His body was too sensitive to hers, and he doubted that that would change anytime soon.

Viva quietly asked, "Do you really think that's such a good idea?"

He tried to muster a smile, but in the end he simply grimaced. "Probably not, but I'll make the best of it."

"I don't want to be tempted."

Spence cleared his throat. "I already am."

"So am I," she confessed.

Startled by her admission, he suspected that his surprise showed in his face. "Then why fight it?"

"I don't want to make a mistake."

That hurt, he realized. "Is that how you think of me? As a potential mistake?"

She shook her head. "Of course not. It's just that . . ." Her voice trailed off.

"It's just what?" he pressed, gathering her into his heat and abandoning his battle to control his desire.

"I don't like starting things I can't finish."

"We could make it work, Viva. We could make us work."

"How can you be so sure?"

"I'm not sure, but I think we're both worth the effort involved in finding out."

"A bicoastal love affair?" she asked. "Not very practical, especially considering our individual schedules."

"It would be a place to start."

"What if we destroy our friendship by becoming lovers?"

What's happening between us is a hell of a lot more than the start of a casual affair.

As stunning as that thought was, Spence didn't articulate it. He needed to come to terms with the reality that he might be falling in love with Viva Conrad, longtime friend and newly acquired partner. And he felt confident that Viva wasn't ready for a discussion about the future. From his vantage point, the present was enough of a problem for her.

"I don't see how that would happen," he said quietly. "We've weathered a lot of storms together over the years."

She exhaled, then rested her forehead against his chin. "I want you, Spence, more than I think you realize, but the timing . . ."

"Timing isn't the point, either," he insisted.

"How can you be so sure?"

"Instinct. Pure instinct."

"And what do your instincts tell you about me?" she asked after several moments.

"Dangerous question," he cautioned her warily. "Are you sure you want an answer?"

"Probably not," she conceded, sounding exhausted and lonely and too fragile for words.

He hated the dejection he heard in her voice. "Does your hesitation have anything to do with the fact that you were engaged to my stepbrother?"

She glanced up at him. "Not in the way you mean."

Yet another indirect answer to a direct question, he thought to himself. Concealing his annoyance, he asked, "Then what's holding you back?"

"It's complicated."

"Life's complicated, Viva, but we all manage to survive the roller-coaster ride. We adapt. We make compromises. We work hard, and we say thank you for the infrequent but very special private moments that feed our emotional needs."

"Sometimes compromise isn't possible."

"Then we make it possible."

"You can't control everything, Spence," she said heatedly.

"I don't want to control you. I want to make love to you."

Viva paled. "You don't know what you're suggesting," she whispered.

"Explain it to me then, because I'm more than willing to listen."

"I can't."

Her stress was too obvious to ignore, so he didn't persist. "Why don't you get into bed? I can let myself out."

"I need to reactivate the alarm."

"You've become the poster child for stubbornness, haven't you?" In total frustration, he picked her up, cradled her against his chest, and carried her out of the kitchen. "I need directions."

"At the far end of the hallway," she said in a subdued voice before she added more forcefully, "And I'm not a child, so quit trying to parent me."

"You can tell me how to activate the system after I tuck you in for the night." He glanced down at her. "I know you're not a child."

"All right." She looped her arms around his neck and rested her head on his shoulder. "See that you don't forget."

"Trust me, I'm not about to forget."

Spence carried her into the master suite of the hilltop estate. After settling her on the bed and removing her slippers, he drew the covers over her legs and plumped her pillows. He noticed the bemused expression on her face when he straightened. As he peered down at her, he fought the urge to shed his clothing and join her.

"Thank you, Doctor Hammond."

"You're welcome." Beneath his gruffness lurked his humor.

She grinned. "You can still make me laugh."

"Then consider me your own personal court jester." He sat down beside her, aware of the risks involved. Spence took her hands, pressed his palms to hers, and wove his fingers through her more slender ones.

"I used to think of you as my own personal

knight in slightly tarnished armor when I was a little girl."

"So that's why you acted like my shadow. Every time I looked up, there you were with those big baby blues flashing sparks at me."

"I didn't approve of your girlfriends. They were all over you, kind of like white on rice."

He laughed, savoring this glimpse of the light-hearted girl he'd once known. Leaning forward, he dropped a hard little kiss on her lips.

Her smile faded as she brought a fingertip to her lips and touched the spot he'd kissed. "That's not a good idea, Spence," she warned softly. "You should leave now."

"I'm not making any moves on you. I just want you to know that you're not alone."

Viva shook her head, her expression determined. "In the final analysis, everyone's alone."

"Not unless we choose to be."

She squeezed his hand, then released it. "Drive carefully. I'll check in with you tomorrow about the paperwork you brought over tonight."

He chuckled, but it sounded strained. "Some things never change."

"Like what?"

"Your famous work ethic." He paused, then asked, "How about a hug?"

She didn't say anything for a long moment. "I could use one more," she finally admitted.

"Me, too, little one. Me too."

He drew her into his arms. She eased into his

embrace with the naturalness of a steadily advancing tide, then molded herself to him in a way that made his heart swell and threaten to burst. He cared more about her than he could have expressed at that particular moment.

"I've missed you." She whispered the words against the side of his neck. "So much."

He heard each word and the sigh that followed. Her admission, coupled with the stark look of loneliness in her extraordinary blue eyes when he eased her backward, combined to swamp his good intentions. He gathered her close on the heels of the tremor—a tremor born not of fear, but of desire, he suspected—that moved through her. His body responded, his bloodstream igniting like torched fuel. The tightening in his loins served notice that he'd never been hungrier for a woman.

As though reading the cover page from the book that was his soul, she urged, "You'd better go now."

He cupped her cheek with the palm of his hand. And he wondered how in hell he was supposed to walk away from her.

"Please, Spence, for both our sakes."

He reluctantly nodded. "You're right." He didn't move a muscle, though, nor did he remove his hand from her cheek.

She turned her head and pressed a kiss into the center of his palm. "I'll be all right. You don't have to worry about me."

He felt the impact of her lips and her warm

breath in the depths of his soul. "I know you'll be okay." *I plan to make sure you are*, he silently vowed. No one harms you, Viva Conrad. No one. Not ever.

"I'll probably spend most of the weekend resting."

"And eating properly?"

"And eating properly," she promised with a faint smile.

"Houghton's party is tomorrow night," he reminded her, delaying the inevitability of his departure.

"I know. The answer to your question is yes. I'm planning to attend."

"I'll pick you up."

"I'll meet you there," she countered. "There's no point in your driving all the way down the coast only to make the return trip twice in one night. Besides, I don't know how long I'll stay, and I don't want to cut your evening short."

"It doesn't matter."

"It matters," she disagreed. "With the auction next week, you'll want to talk business with some of the other owners."

"You're well informed."

She lifted and lowered her shoulders in a shrug. "I pay attention when it counts."

He leaned forward then, unable to resist the sheer temptation of the laughter dancing in her eyes and his memory of the lushness of her lips, lips he needed to taste once more, although he knew he was indulging in a form of self-torture.

"Spence . . . ," she whispered on a sigh.

"That's my name," he answered before he brushed his lips lightly over hers.

He deliberately tantalized her senses by trailing the tip of his tongue along the seam of her trembling lips, and then he bathed her full lower lip with moisture before he worried it with a careful teething motion. She responded, coming alive with a suddenness that caught him off guard.

Spence celebrated her uninhibitedness when Viva parted her lips and angled her head. When he thrust his tongue into the sultry heat of her mouth, her tongue instantly tangled with his.

He felt the tremor that worked its way through her when she edged closer and aligned her upper body to his. He stroked her back as he plundered her mouth, and she melted against him even more. Her breasts plumped enticingly against his chest, the taut nipples defined despite her robe.

Spence, his respiration uneven, resisted the impulse to peel her robe away from her shapely body and expose her nakedness. He didn't want to hurry or overwhelm her. More than anything, he wanted to take his time with her.

Viva moaned, then undulated against him. Caught up in the sensations raging like a brush fire through his entire body, Spence felt his control unravel even more. He surrendered to the heat and hunger driving him, helpless to resist Viva's responsiveness.

Their kisses intensified. Their hands glided and skimmed, moving in deliberate exploration, then with escalating franticness, over the curves and hollows of each other's bodies.

Spence traced the line of her spine and spanned her narrow waist with his fingertips before he bracketed her hips between his palms. The heat of her skin sank into his pores in spite of the silk that covered her from throat to ankles. Although he hesitated briefly, he couldn't resist the need to shift his hands forward and cup her breasts.

Viva groaned, and he savored the sound as he closed his hands over her and caressed her. When her nipples tightened to small knots, he tugged at them. She arched under his skillful touch, and an inarticulate murmur escaped her. She pulled back and stared up at him.

Spence watched her in the muted light provided by a small bedside lamp. Breathless and flushed, she was everything he wanted, everything he desired, would ever desire.

"What are you thinking?" he asked, unable to stop himself from peeling apart the bodice of her robe and exposing her high, full breasts to his gaze.

"I need you," she answered, sounding as shaken as he felt. "So much."

Her honesty reached into his heart and humbled him. Ducking his head, he licked the tip of one of her breasts. She clutched his head with both hands, then released a sharp breath of shock and pleasure as he drew the taut peak deeply into his mouth and suckled her.

After several minutes, he met her gaze. Filling his hands with her swollen breasts, he stroked his thumbs back and forth across the distended tips. "I need you too. More than I've ever needed anyone."

Her eyes widened, but she said nothing. She watched him while she placed her hands atop his muscular thighs. She kneaded the muscular terrain like a she-cat, methodically working her way up his thighs, her fingertips moving in ever-expanding circles.

Spence almost stopped breathing when she paused. He waited, though, waited for Viva to decide if the path she'd chosen was the right one for her. He trusted the instinct that urged him not to voice a single word of urging. He left the choice about what would or would not happen between them to her.

She glanced down, studying the position of her fingers, which were poised just centimeters from his swollen groin. Then she looked at Spence.

He reached out, belatedly noticing that his hand shook as he threaded his fingers through the denseness of her long hair. "Do you want to stop?"

"No."

"You can call a halt to this at any time. You do know that, don't you?"

Viva nodded, then scooted forward. She fitted her hands over him. As she stroked him through the fabric of his trousers, she said, "I know, Spence, but that's not going to happen."

"Will you be as certain tomorrow that what occurs between us tonight is right?" he asked despite the torturous pleasure of her caressing fingertips. "I don't want you to feel regret, because this . . . this is a beginning for us, Viva, not just some accident of fate."

He wouldn't have hesitated with any other woman, but with Viva he couldn't just settle for one night in her bed. He wanted and needed more. Much more.

She paused to search his features with a troubled gaze. "I'll deal with tomorrow when it arrives."

He frowned, but she gave him no options in the seconds that followed. She continued to fondle him, her boldness making him feel as though his body would soon detonate if she persisted, but he wanted her hands on him. He craved the unexpected eroticism of her touch and her nature, although these facets of her personality were new to him.

"I wouldn't hurt you for the world, Viva."

She smiled. "I've always known that about you." She slowly released the buttons of his shirt, then unzipped his trousers.

Spence basked in the pleasure her light touch provoked as she traced the pattern of dark hair that arrowed downward from his chest to his loins. Her fingers suddenly dipped, and she freed his throbbing flesh.

Drawing in enough air to feed his lungs, he gloried in the incendiary bursts of sensation exploding within him as she measured the length and thickness of his sex with gliding fingertips. He freed the tie of her robe with shaking hands and smoothed the silk away from her body. The fabric pooled at her hips.

He watched her smile and heard the almost melodic sigh that passed her lips as he caressed her breasts. After a battle for self-control, he slowly trailed his knuckles down the front of her body. When he slid his fingers into the black silk at the top of her thighs, he discovered the quivering wet heat of her secret feminine flesh.

Viva trembled violently, but she didn't make any move to distance herself from his exploring touch. She continued to stroke his hardness, her fingertips provoking yet another riot of sensations within him.

Inspired by her response, he glided his fingers along the swollen folds of her body before slipping two fingers into her. He immediately felt the internal quiver that seized her. He loved her reaction, just as he loved the heated essence of her passion.

He penetrated her over and over again with his fingers, his thumb simultaneously skimming back and forth across the nubbin of sensitive flesh concealed from view. He tested her body's resilience and slick heat, thoroughly acquainting himself with her innate sensuality as he aroused her.

She clutched at his shoulders and her eyes fluttered closed. She trembled, as though battered by a powerful wind, and small sounds emerged from her as she repeatedly arched into his touch.

Although desperately hungry to join their bodies in the ultimate act of intimacy, he continued to pleasure her, finding his own pleasure enhanced by the act of giving rather than taking the relief his body clamored for.

He deepened his caresses until she gasped and sprawled back against the mound of pillows at the head of the bed. Her sensuality and the heat of her satin-soft skin drove him on. Bending over her, he dropped a string of kisses along every inch of skin he encountered as he made his way down her writhing torso.

When he settled his mouth over her femininity and teased her with leisurely strokes of his tongue, she whimpered, the sound eventually turning into a long low moan that foretold her impending release. She came apart just seconds later, her climax ripping through her and producing a sustained quaking of her body that Spence easily controlled with his strong hands.

He continued to sip from her, determined to prolong her pleasure while also nurturing his own. When Viva slumped against the pillows in exhaustion and exhaled raggedly, he released her, got to his feet, and finished disrobing.

Pushing aside the covers, he joined her in bed. He settled atop her, supporting his upper body weight with his elbows and lodging his lean hips between her parted thighs. Cupping her breasts in his hands, he teased the taut mauve buds with his lips and darting strokes of his tongue.

Shuddering delicately, she opened her eyes and peered at him. "You surprised me," Viva whispered.

He lifted his head and smiled at her. "Good. Expect more of the same."

She trailed her fingertips down the side of his face. "All right."

"I never had a clue, you know."

"About what?" she asked.

"That you were so sexually volatile."

She gave him an impish grin. "Neither did I."

He plucked at the distended nipple of one breast with his fingers while simultaneously leaning down to suckle the other.

She arched under his mouth and fingers, then released a shaky sigh. "Neither did I," she managed a second time.

Her admission and her response spurred him on. He delighted in summoning reactions from her that she'd never experienced before. He took pride in the fact that what they were sharing was different from the other relationships they'd both had in the past.

Spence knew there'd been only two men in her life—a college boyfriend and his stepbrother. Although he didn't want to admit it aloud, he appreciated Viva's conservative dating history for purely selfish reasons. His own was extensive, but he knew his health was excellent.

"I was just thinking about something," he said.

"I can't think at all when you have your mouth and hands on me," she confessed.

He smiled. "Good."

"That sounded vaguely like the male of the species preening over his sexual prowess."

"Sorry."

"You're forgiven," she said, laughter in her voice.

He moved off of her, positioned himself beside her, and drew her into his arms as she reclined on her back. "Back to what I was thinking. I want you to know that you don't have to worry about my health. I haven't been involved with anyone in more than six months, and I've had a thorough checkup recently."

Viva admitted, "Tommy mentioned that you'd put your social life on hold."

Spence chuckled ruefully. "How thoughtful of him."

"He thought of you as family, Spence, and he talked about you a lot, especially during the last few months of his life."

"You were in touch with him?" he asked, surprised.

Viva nodded. "At least once a week after I left. At the end, almost every day."

Spence realized then how off base he'd been about her. "It seems I owe you another apology."

She didn't try to evade his curious gaze. "You couldn't have known. Tommy understood that I needed time for myself, and he promised he wouldn't tell anyone where I was until I gave him the go-ahead."

"Then he knew why you left."

She nodded warily. "Yes."

"But you still aren't ready to tell me, are you?"

"I don't want to talk about it right now, Spence."

"You will eventually, though."

"Eventually," she confirmed.

"All right," he said, aware that any pressure he brought to bear on her now would be construed as manipulation. He refused to indulge in such tactics in a sexually charged situation, despite his frustration with the secrets Viva insisted on keeping. "I should have known that you wouldn't turn your back on Tommy."

"He never turned his back on me," she reminded him as she freed herself from his embrace and sat up.

After pushing her hair out of her face, she nudged him onto his back and slipped astride him with the finesse of a jockey mounting a Thoroughbred.

"Back in the saddle again, I see, Ms. Conrad," he teased as he gripped her squirming hips and stilled her movement.

Laughing, she leaned forward and nipped at his chin. "No pun intended, Mr. Hammond?"

His body surged with as yet unappeased desire when she shifted her hips. "Careful. My control where you're concerned is iffy, at best."

"You're the epitome of control." She grinned at him. "You're known for your control in some circles."

"I'm on the verge of having none . . ." He sucked in a harsh breath as she reached behind her, clasped him snugly with one hand, and stroked him ever so slowly. He felt sparks of sensation cascade through his body like hot flecks of glitter. "None . . . what . . . so . . . ever," he said with a groan.

"I like touching you." She spoke in a low seductive tone of voice that incinerated his senses.

He realized yet again that he'd never thought of her as a sensual being, but she was that and more. Spence shuddered, the up-and-down motion of her hand doing major damage to his dwindling control. "I like being touched by you," he responded before he slid his hand to her nape. He tugged her closer, but without dislodging her stroking hand. "I like it a hell of a lot."

She sighed.

He felt her warm breath wash across his throat before she lifted her head. He met her gaze. "Tell me what you want," he ordered in a desire-ravaged voice.

Viva smiled. "You're getting awfully bossy in your old age."

"Tell me."

"First, I want your mouth."

"Then take it," he challenged.

She did, indulging in a long, utterly voracious exploration of his mouth until she grew breathless. She relinquished his lips, then told him, "I want something else now."

He pinned her with an incendiary look. "So do I."

Viva straightened. She let her head drift to one side. Her eyes fell closed. She increased the stroking motion of her hand.

Spence ground his jaws together, his control hanging by a thread. "Viva . . . ," he began, unaware that his grip on her hips was in danger of causing fingerprint bruises.

"I want to feel you inside me." She whispered the words as she swayed atop him.

"You can have whatever you want," he managed, lifting her easily.

Positioned on her knees, she tugged on his wrists. He cooperated as she drew them away from her hips and shifted his hands so that they were positioned above his head. Leaning forward, her hips poised just inches above his engorged shaft, she simultaneously pressed her palms over his, claimed his mouth in a scintillating kiss, and slowly began to impale herself with his hardness.

Spence groaned, the heat and tightness of her

body like a scalding glove around his flesh. He gripped her hands, his hips arching as she took him as deeply within herself as her body would allow.

Viva sighed, her insides clenching and un-clenching around Spence's maleness. "You feel so good."

"You're deliberately torturing me," he half accused.

"Shall I stop?" she asked.

"Never," he answered. "Dear God, never."

She began to ride him in a rhythm as old as time. He opened his eyes a few minutes later, still struggling with the shocked sense of rightness streaming through his consciousness and his utter certainty that he'd finally found his true emotional home, to see the last thing he ever expected to see.

Stunned to discover that Viva was weeping soundlessly as their bodies mated, Spence surged upward atop the mattress to a seated position. He smoothed her legs around his hips and encircled her shaking form in a fiercely protective embrace without breaking the union of their bodies.

SIX

"Have I hurt you?" he asked, his alarm evident.

Viva shook her head and swiped at the tears streaking her cheeks. Too embarrassed to speak, she buried her face in the curve of his neck.

"Viva, for God's sake, tell me what's wrong."

"Nothing's wrong," she insisted in a choked voice.

He gently eased her into view, then cradled her cheek in the palm of his hand. "Open your eyes and look at me," Spence said.

Reluctantly meeting his gaze, she grappled with the feelings he evoked. She felt utterly swamped by emotions and sensations too far-reaching to define. Especially now.

Tears threatened anew, but she fought them. She loved him so much, she realized, that she was trembling, inside and out, from the shock of having her fantasies about him suddenly turned into such a stunning reality.

"Tell me why you're crying?"

After taking a calming breath, she mustered a watery smile. "My emotions are a little out of whack, that's all. I'm fine. Really."

His reluctance to accept her explanation showed in his facial features. "Talk to me, Viva."

She sagged in his embrace, suddenly defeated by his concern and the myriad of emotions crashing around inside of her. "I've never wanted a man so much that I'm shaking from the desire I feel."

"And," he encouraged quietly.

"And I'm feeling emotions I've never felt while making love." She shook her head, not quite believing the things she was saying to him. "You must think I'm insane."

"That's all?"

"Yes," she whispered.

"You're sure?" he pressed.

"Spence, I'm sure. Please stop grilling me."

"I thought I'd injured you. I couldn't control how much I wanted you. I needed to be inside you. And if you're insane, then so am I," he added almost as an afterthought.

She shook her head. "You didn't hurt me. You just made me feel . . ." She paused, searching for the right words.

"What?" he asked.

"So much. Like I was being submerged in sensations. That's never happened to me before."

"Did I frighten you?"

Frighten? She laughed softly. "Hardly. I liked . . . loved," Viva amended, "everything. It's what I dreamed it would be like with you." She shrugged. "Are you shocked?"

"That you've had fantasies?" He chuckled. "Hell, no. I've had plenty of my own to contend with where you're concerned."

She didn't question how long he'd indulged his imagination with erotic thoughts, because then he might ask her the same question. To have to admit that she'd wanted him as a lover for nearly two years wasn't something she intended to do.

He grinned at her. "We're a pair, aren't we? Old enough to know what we want, but not too well informed about each other beyond a friendship we've both taken for granted. I wonder what a shrink would make of us?"

"I don't think I want to know," Viva remarked.

She welcomed the hard hug he gave her a moment later. Molded against his sturdy frame, she felt the throbbing strength of his arousal, which was still imbedded in her body. Her nipples tingled and tightened, and desire that resembled shooting flames traveled through her bloodstream at a breakneck pace.

She sensed and felt his relief that he hadn't physically injured her as much of the tension in his broad shoulders eased beneath her fingertips. He was a large man, and generously endowed. Viva knew now that he was a man who was wise enough and sensitive enough to temper his physical prowess with concern for the well-being of his partner.

"You aren't alone, you know," he finally said once he eased backward again.

"You feel overwhelmed too?"

Spence nodded. "It was more than I expected. More than I was prepared for. You are more than I expected. You're a shock, pure and simple."

"You're not sorry we've done this, are you?" she asked as she smoothed a lock of dark hair off his brow.

His maleness pulsed within the snug channel of her body and the hands gripping her hips tightened. "What do you think?"

She trembled. "I don't want to think. I just want to feel," she said, nibbling at his neck with hungry lips as her hands shifted across the width of his shoulders and swept down his back. "I want to focus on us, and I want to share everything possible with you."

He groaned as she squirmed atop him. "Greedy little imp, aren't you?"

Leaning back, she looked at him. The intensity she glimpsed in his eyes prompted her admission, "Where you're concerned, I doubt my appetite will ever be satisfied."

She wondered in the next heartbeat if she'd said too much, perhaps even revealed the depth of her love. She couldn't help wondering if, under other circumstances, he would even want to know the extent of her feelings for him. She knew she wasn't fearless enough to risk a thorough confession, so she bit her tongue when the impulse persisted.

"You aren't alone, Viva." Spence spoke with a tenderness that was reflected in his touch as he framed her face with his hands.

Relief flooded her. "I don't feel alone anymore."

"You never have been," he told her. "And you never will be. I promise."

Viva appreciated his effort to reassure her, but she knew better. The course she'd set for herself was a solitary one, and she couldn't afford to forget it. She realized that what they now shared was a stolen moment in time, and it had to remain a secret. No one could know. No one.

Unwilling to dwell on her sad thoughts, she pressed a quick kiss to his lips, then smoothed a single fingertip across his chin. "Have I told you that I like the way you kiss?"

He looked amused by her question. "I'm not sure, but you can tell me again if you'd like."

"I love the way you taste. And I especially love the way you touch me." She shifted forward, her breasts pushing against the hard wall of his chest, the soft curve of her belly nudging against the washboard ridges of his abdomen.

"I'll second that."

Viva twisted against him, instinctively seeking relief from the hunger that dominated her consciousness. "I want you," she said. "Don't make me wait."

In one smooth motion Spence separated their bodies, lifted her, and eased her into a reclining position. Coming down over her, he thrust into her. "Your wish is my command."

Viva caught her breath, then exhaled shakily as he settled even more deeply into her. Circling his hips with her legs, she gripped his shoulders.

Their bodies united once again, they stared at each other. The world faded. Time ceased to be a concept worthy of consideration. Adversaries disappeared. Problems seemed almost suspended.

"Love me, Spence," she whispered. "Please make love to me." *Make me forget,* she finished silently as she gazed up at him, *if only for a little while.*

She felt his maleness surge with power in the moments that followed, as though in direct response to her plea. She felt as well the possessiveness of his embrace as he gathered her even closer. She moaned her approval and her relief as he set a reckless pace.

Viva met his every thrust with a counterthrust and twisting motion of her hips that sent shock waves of sensation through both their bodies. Spence claimed her mouth with the same intensity of purpose evident in the driving motion of his hips.

Her insides tightened into knots of tension. She surrendered completely to their mating, the sense of oneness with him that she felt unlike anything she'd ever experienced before.

"Let yourself go, Viva," Spence urged as their bodies slammed together.

She gasped, twisting against him in anticipation of release. She declared her love and made a gift of her heart without giving voice to the words she longed to say to him.

And then she lost total control.

Spence drove her to the brink of mindlessness, then hurled her over the edge of an invisible precipice. She screamed without realizing it, her climax so far-reaching and sustained that she flirted with a loss of consciousness.

Gentling his pace, Spence refrained from seeking his own release. He continued to hold her and rock against her, ever so gently penetrating her body while also allowing her time to regain some sense of herself and her surroundings.

Viva finally opened her eyes, too dazed in the wake of his sensual generosity to speak at first. Her body quivered internally, then slowly eased into an answering rhythmic motion as a result of the subtle movement of Spence's hips.

He smiled at her despite the strain that enhanced the angular contours of his face.

"More," she said on a sigh. "I want more."

He thrust deeply into her, then paused as a tremor racked his entire body.

Viva sucked in a startled breath as her body accustomed itself once more to his size and the depth of his penetration. Escalating desire swept through her yet again.

"How do you feel right now?" he asked.

She knew he wasn't being coy or asking to be graded. "Wonderful."

"I'm glad." He dipped into her with studied deliberation.

"You're holding back." She punctuated her comment with an upward motion of her pelvis.

He stiffened in response to her less than subtle movement, his eyes briefly closing before he refocused on her. "Is that a problem?"

Smiling, she shook her head and tugged him closer. Capturing his lips, she duplicated his probing exploration of her lower body with her thrusting tongue. She slipped it past his lips and teeth to explore the ridges and hollows beyond. When he sucked at the tip of her tongue, the delicate inner muscles of her lower body clenched around him.

He muttered against her lips, "No fair."

"All's fair . . ." Viva didn't finish the sentence. She didn't dare risk it, because she knew she was in danger of telling Spence how much she loved him. Instead, she ducked her head and trailed a string of stinging little kisses along the column of his neck before whispering in his ear, "I want to feel you come."

He threw back his head, then shuddered in response to her starkly erotic comment. "Only if you join me," he bartered through gritted teeth before another tremor rippled through him.

She felt his response all the way to the marrow

of her bones. She adored it, just as she adored him. "Now," Viva demanded breathlessly.

"Say please," he answered, stubborn to the end.

Smiling, she shifted her hips enticingly. Pleasure rushed through her like a river running pell-mell over the edge of a cliff. She felt the throbbing fullness of his sex, and basked in the richness of emotion that accompanied his possession.

"Now," she said again. "Please."

He plunged deeply, withdrew partway, then plunged again. Over and over. Clinging to him, Viva rode out the erotic storm that swept over them, giving even as she received, indulging her senses and her heart in the most exquisite shared journey of her adult life.

Spence took her on a whirlwind tour of pure sensation. He pursued a punishing pace. As her body tightened into itself, he pushed Viva with a relentlessness that forced her to embrace not simply his physical intensity but a release that shattered her with the force of detonating dynamite.

She gripped his hips as she started to unravel inside, and then cried out as her climax assaulted her senses like an exploding starburst. Convulsive aftershocks followed.

Viva didn't slow her movement, though. Instead, she matched Spence thrust for thrust as her release tremored through her. She said his name, repeatedly, in a passion-induced mantra that expressed love and desire and dreams shadowed by the threat of death if the future went awry.

And then she prayed as she held tightly to him as he followed her into the breach. She prayed for the future.

He gasped her name in the same instant that his release began. He continued to surge into her, the force of his climax sending shock waves through his powerful frame.

As she held him close and felt him spend his passion within the confines of her body, Viva knew that she would never love a man as completely as she loved Spencer Hammond. He was her destiny, the mate of her heart and soul. Without him, she would always be incomplete. But if she followed her emotions and indulged herself, he might be killed.

Clinging to each other in the aftermath of their passion, they collapsed across the bed in a sweaty, limb-tangled sprawl. The only sound in the room for quite some time was their ragged breathing.

Would they have more than this one night? Viva wondered as Spence held her. She knew the hurtful answer, even though she longed to pretend otherwise. Tears brimmed in her eyes. Determined not to weep, she blinked them back.

Her heart shattered as she fought the desire to be selfish, fought the impulse to damn the consequences and accept Spence's certainty that they could share an intimate relationship as the future unfolded. They couldn't chance it, though. Viva resented the task she faced once the dawn arrived.

Rejecting Spence was the last thing she wanted to do, although she realized it was inevitable.

Spence shifted their still-joined bodies to one side a short while later, but he kept Viva cradled against his broad chest. She savored his strength and their closeness.

Although she was exhausted, she didn't let herself drift off. As Spence dozed, Viva imprinted every passing second she spent in his embrace onto her senses, storing up the memory of each precious moment and fighting the dread that accompanied the coming dawn.

After showering, shaving, and dressing the next morning, Spence left the master suite and made his way to the kitchen. He spotted Viva when he glanced outside. She stood at the railing of the back deck.

He paused to study her, his mind producing a home movie of the previous night. His memories generated a rush of white-hot heat through his veins and the awareness that he'd never wanted a woman more than he wanted Viva. He realized that she had become as essential to his survival as life-sustaining oxygen.

Clad in a white silk caftan, her feet bare, and her long hair teased by the buffeting summer morning breeze, Viva reminded him of a painting he'd discovered in a Paris art gallery of a woman poised atop a windswept bluff that overlooked the azure waters of the Mediterranean.

He'd purchased the painting and placed it in his office, although the cost had been exorbitant. He hadn't been able to resist the painting, any more than he'd been able to resist Viva.

Like the painting, Viva provoked sensual fantasies.

Like the painting, Viva always seemed just beyond his grasp.

Like Viva, who took his breath away even now, the woman in the painting gave the appearance and impression of total inaccessibility.

She turned to look at him as he approached her.

His stride normally a reflection of his assertive personality, Spence's footsteps briefly faltered when he noticed the hint of melancholy lurking behind her smile. "Why the long face?" he asked, his tone purposefully light as he paused beside her.

"What do you mean?"

"You look as if you're waiting for the executioner."

She wrinkled her nose at him. "You're imagining things. How about some coffee? It should be ready by now."

She started to walk past him, but he caught her hand. "The coffee can wait, Viva."

"All right." She gave him a curious look. "Problem?" she asked.

He tugged her forward, reeling her into his

arms so that their bodies were perfectly aligned. "After last night, I would hope not."

She looped her arms around his waist and held on to him with the kind of fierceness that reminded him of a drowning victim clinging to a life preserver. As she rested her forehead against his chin, she exhaled shakily.

Spence frowned. Didn't she understand how much she meant to him, or did she think that he considered what they'd shared little more than a romp in the sack between two consenting adults? he wondered.

Even though he hadn't had the time to examine all of the ramifications of the change in their relationship, he knew in his heart that his life would never be the same. Hers, either, if he had anything to say about it.

"Second thoughts?" he asked quietly, prepared to deal with them.

She shook her head, eased backward in his embrace without separating their bodies, and peered up at him. "None."

"Regrets?" he persisted, not really believing her and determined to understand her state of mind.

"No."

"Right answers." But the wrong tone of voice, he amended silently as he studied her.

"What about you?" she asked after a moment of hesitation.

"Absolutely none." He stroked the side of her

face with his fingertips as he dropped a kiss on the tip of her nose. "Last night was . . ."

She shifted closer, burrowing against his body in a playfully suggestive way that reminded him of the spontaneity of her passion. "Last night . . . ," she prompted.

Spence cleared his throat as his body throbbed with renewed desire. ". . . was nothing short of amazing. Kind of like you."

She grinned up at him. "I am?"

"Trust me."

"I guess I should," she teased. "You're the one with all the experience."

Sobering, Spence studied her. "Is that what's bothering you? My rather diverse past?"

"Should it?"

"No. This is now, Viva. And the future."

Her grin disappeared, and she looked away.

He nudged her face back into view with his fingertips. "We've wasted a lot of years."

She ducked free of his touch and shook her head. "I don't agree."

That surprised and disappointed him. "Why?"

"It wouldn't have worked before. It still might not, despite what we both think we want in the future."

He seized her by the waist and held her still when she started to move away from him. "Last night was a beginning."

"We can't be sure of that, Spence."

"I am. I'm very sure," he said stubbornly.

"Such clarity of vision, Mr. Hammond. I envy you."

"I know what I want."

"So do I," she answered. Sadness tinged her smile. "But what we want and what we get are often poles apart. It is definitely time for some coffee."

"You do that a lot, you know."

"What do I do?"

"You pretend to misunderstand me, or you verbally sidestep me if I get too close to a subject you find uncomfortable."

Viva shrugged.

His gaze narrowed, he noticed the tension in her features despite her seemingly casual gesture.

"Some things are better left unsaid," she cautioned.

She evaded his attempt to waylay her a second time, then crossed the wide deck to the entrance of the kitchen. Spence followed her. As he stepped into the kitchen, he noticed that she'd already set the table for a light breakfast of fresh fruit, croissants, juice, and coffee.

Glancing at him, she flashed a bright smile his way. One of those brittle smiles that he recognized as a sign of stress in Viva. He felt his heart sink a little more.

"I don't know about you, but I'm starved," she said.

He didn't comment one way or another as she extracted the carafe from the coffeemaker and carried it to the table. Taking a seat after she filled two mugs with the steaming black brew, she reached for the juice glass at her place setting and took a sip.

She met his gaze. "Aren't you hungry?"

Spence took the chair opposite her, silently noting that she'd positioned him out of reaching distance. He suspected that her behavior was deliberate. He also sensed that she was having second thoughts about their night together, despite her comment to the contrary. He didn't understand why, though.

Not once had Viva given him any hint that she questioned the passion they'd shared. And he knew her well enough to realize that she'd never been casual about intimacy. Unless her emotions were involved, she wasn't the kind of woman to indulge in sex as a form of exercise for her libido.

For him, their night had been filled with revelations. A night of sensory awareness fueled by Viva's remarkably sensual nature. A night replete with the kind of emotional satisfaction that enhanced and exceeded the physical a thousand times over.

He'd lost track of how many times they'd made love, but he knew he wouldn't ever forget the stunning eroticism of the hours they'd spent together. No woman had ever aroused him more. No woman had ever made him feel more male. And no woman had ever simultaneously claimed his heart and body during the act of making love. Until last night.

Spence wondered then if Viva grasped the impact she'd had on him. He still felt somewhat overwhelmed by the diverse emotions she evoked, and he wasn't quite ready to delve too deeply into them just yet.

With the women he'd dated over the years, he'd always remained emotionally aloof, never permitting anyone to get too close. He'd deliberately avoided investing himself in a permanent relationship. Instead, he'd told himself that it was enough to raise his daughter and pursue his professional goals, but now he realized that he'd been living in an emotional vacuum.

With Viva he'd experienced feelings he hadn't allowed himself to feel since his first marriage. Although on many levels he trusted those feelings, he needed to accustom himself to the newness of them.

Besides, he silently reasoned, it was too soon to speak of the future with Viva when so many unanswered questions about the last fourteen months stood between them.

As he sat across from her, Spence realized that she was the perfect lover—profoundly sensual, instinctively curious, and open to diversity. She held nothing back. She simply gave, inspiring complex responses whether or not she realized it. She also gave new meaning to the timeworn cliché about still waters running very deep.

Spence knew he needed time to think through the last ten hours. So did Viva, but now he wondered if she would give them both the time they required. In spite of her assurances, he sensed that she regretted, at least in ways he didn't understand, the intimacy of the previous night. He hoped he was wrong, but he doubted it.

"Are you ready to tell me what's bothering you?" he asked quietly, ignoring the instincts clamoring inside him to proceed cautiously with her.

"I'm a little tired." She managed a faint smile. "We didn't get much sleep last night."

"No, we didn't," Spence conceded.

"I'll probably take a nap once you leave."

"In a hurry to get rid of me?"

Viva blanched. "Of course not."

Spence pushed aside his plate, which held an uneaten croissant. "You could have fooled me. I feel about as welcome right now as the plague."

"Spence . . ." Her voice broke. She swallowed convulsively. She fumbled for her juice glass and succeeded in knocking it over.

He tossed his napkin atop the puddle to stop it from spreading. "What's going on with you?"

She stared at the soaked napkin for several moments, then glanced at him. "I guess I'm more tired than I realized."

"Dammit, Viva!" he shouted as he surged to his feet.

She slowly pushed up from her chair. "Don't ruin last night, please."

"That's not what I'm doing."

"Isn't it?" she whispered so softly that he almost didn't hear her question.

He grasped the top rung of his chair with both

hands in order to keep himself from seizing her bodily and hauling her back to the master suite. "You're shutting me out again, and I want to know why."

"I think you should leave now, Spence."

"I'm not going anywhere."

Her chin came up a notch. "Last night was wonderful, but . . . it's over."

"I'm dismissed, is that it? Just like that?"

"You aren't being dismissed, and you know it. We're both adults, Spence. We needed each other, and it was beautiful. I meant it when I said I didn't have any regrets, but we both have to move forward with our lives now."

Convinced that he had no choice, he abruptly demanded, "Why did you run after Michael's funeral?"

Staggering slightly, she grabbed the edge of the table for support. "I told you I wouldn't—"

He broke in, discarding the ingrained good manners of a lifetime because he sensed that he was fighting for them both now. "Shall I tell you what *I* know?"

She shook her head. "Don't bother. I don't want to hear it."

"You're gonna hear it, even if I have to nail you to that chair to get you to listen to me."

"Don't threaten me."

"I'll do anything I damn well please when you act this way."

"I'm not acting. I have nothing more to say to

you, so please stop this now before you destroy both of us with your persistent questions."

"Destroy? That's a hell of a word."

"Go, Spence. Now," she pleaded. "Last night meant more to me than you'll ever know, but it's all we can have."

"You trusted me with your body. Why aren't you willing to trust me with your secrets?" he asked, his voice and his frustration under wraps for the moment.

"I can't." She raised a shaking hand and pressed her fingertips to her temple. After a long moment she squared her shoulders and looked at him, all expression gone from her face. "I can't, Spence."

The finality in her tone of voice felt like the blow of a fist against his chest. Spence took a step toward her, needing to touch her, needing to remind her of what they'd meant to each other as lovers. Needing *her*.

She backed up, using her chair as a barrier to thwart his advance.

He hesitated. "Viva, you're not behaving rationally."

"I'm doing what I have to do," she insisted.

"I don't understand what's happened to you."

"I know that," she said softly. "But you have to trust me now, because I care too much about you to give you the answers you want."

She wasn't making any sense as far as he was concerned. There was strength in unity. He knew that from personal experience. Although he hated admitting it to himself, Spence recognized the pointlessness of trying to intimidate Viva into opening up. She was exhausted and even more stubborn than he'd ever imagined, and his temper was on the verge of incinerating them both. Despite the difficulty of the task, he forced himself to step back, literally and figuratively.

"We aren't finished with this," he told her, his voice as somber as his emotions.

She slumped against the chair and tears filled her eyes, but she didn't say a word.

Spence turned on his heel and strode out of the kitchen. As he made his way to his car and left the hilltop estate, he vowed that he wouldn't rest until he had the truth and Viva was firmly ensconced in his life. He considered those two issues nonnegotiable. He knew that to pretend otherwise was a waste of time. He loved her too much now. And he needed her.

SEVEN

Although she doubted the wisdom of attending the private party being hosted by friends the weekend prior to Del Mar's legendary Pacific Classic Race, Viva knew she couldn't continue to ignore the social aspects of her responsibilities as an owner. She accepted the invitation, despite the trepidation she felt.

She'd already missed the Houghtons' party, pleading a sudden case of stomach flu, and she'd avoided the Thoroughbred auction. Even though Spence hadn't reappeared on her doorstep to question her absences, Viva sensed that he would fairly soon.

Ten days had passed since their night together. Ten long days and nights steeped in regret and sadness.

She'd spotted Spence at least a half-dozen times during her periodic visits to the stable area for meetings with Ben or to the track's backstretch to observe the early morning workouts. At first she'd felt a certain amount of relief that Spence hadn't tried to confront her, but only until she realized that he was deliberately avoiding her. Viva grew more lonely and frightened with each passing day.

Silence from Spence tautened her nerves to the point of snapping, because she knew that he was searching for answers, in his own way and on his own terms. She feared that he wouldn't relent until he found them, and that fear undermined what little peace of mind she still possessed.

On Saturday evening Viva prepared for the party with great care. After giving herself a facial and manicuring her nails, she indulged in a leisurely soak in the tub. Once she dried her hair, she fashioned it into an elegant chignon and then applied her makeup, the latter an attempt to conceal the smudges of fatigue beneath her eyes and the hollows in her cheeks from losing additional weight.

She dressed in a simple white silk sheath, matching silk stockings, and low-heeled pumps, then added to her ensemble the diamond earrings and a diamond pendant that Uncle Tommy had given to her on her twenty-first birthday. When she inspected herself in the mirror, Viva thought she looked as stressed on the outside as she felt inside. Hardly the appearance she wanted to project, but she knew she'd done her best under the circumstances.

As she left the hilltop estate and made her way to the freeway, she pondered her limited options for dealing with Spence. She couldn't, she realized, avoid a confrontation, but she could be the one to initiate it.

Viva easily located the mansion perched on the edge of the cliff overlooking the Pacific. It was one of several homes owned by the Texas oil magnate and his wife. She remembered that it was filled with an extensive French Impressionists collection that was the envy of several museum curators from across the globe. Normally, she would have appreciated the opportunity to view the paintings once again.

She knew exactly how she would proceed with Spence by the time she gave her car keys to the valet parking attendant. After greeting her host and hostess, she joined the other guests in the sprawling house.

Viva searched the crowd for Spence, the decision she'd made during her thirty-minute drive strengthening her determination to speak to him without delay. She spotted him almost immediately, her heart doing a brisk two-step as she studied him.

Clad in a dark gray silk shirt, black linen trousers, and leather loafers, Spencer Hammond looked as comfortable in the role of successful entrepreneur as he did in the denims and cowboy boots he favored at home.

Viva waited for him to meet her gaze, but when

he did the expression on his hard-angled face revealed nothing of his thoughts. She froze when he subjected her to an impersonal visual once-over, then resumed his conversation with his two companions.

Viva resented his dismissive attitude. It hurt, even if it didn't surprise her. Nothing, she decided yet again as she grappled with her wounded pride, would ever surprise her after the last fourteen months.

Despite her mounting tension, she navigated the crowd in an unhurried manner. She paused often to chat with Kentucky friends and racetrack acquaintances before she finally reached Spence's location on the far side of the room.

The two men with him fell silent at her approach, although both acknowledged her arrival with pleasant smiles of welcome. Spence didn't bother to look at her or to introduce her to the men.

Viva returned the smiles directed her way and stood a little taller. She refused to be ignored. She gripped the small silk-covered purse she carried and kept her voice even as she spoke. "Can I buy you a drink, partner?"

"Excuse me," Spence said to the men. Instead of looking at or responding to Viva, he started to walk away.

Dismayed by his rudeness, Viva caught his arm. She withdrew her hand, though, when she felt him go rigid beneath her fingertips. "Would you join me on the balcony for a few minutes?"

He finally met her gaze. "What's the point?"

The cold look in his eyes almost persuaded her to wait until a better moment. Almost. She knew there would never be a good time for the conversation they were about to have, so she doggedly stayed focused on her purpose for approaching him, in spite of the blow he'd just delivered to her dignity.

"I'd like to talk to you," Viva said, her tone subdued but firm.

"So talk."

"Privately."

Clearly uncomfortable with the unfolding drama in front of them, the two men eyed each other and then drifted away. Viva silently applauded their decision to leave her alone with Spence. She didn't want or need an audience.

"I'm busy, Viva. It'll have to wait."

She shook her head. "No, it can't wait. It's important. Otherwise, I wouldn't bother you."

She tolerated the silence that followed, just as she endured his inspection of her. Chin up and her gaze direct, Viva forced herself to be patient with him, forced herself to keep a tight rein on her temper as his eyes moved over her, although she secretly longed for the warmth and affection they'd shared ten nights earlier.

Spence finally nodded at her, took her arm, and guided her around the clusters of chatting, laughing partygoers. He paused only once at a makeshift bar near the open French doors that led out onto the balcony.

"Do you want anything?" he asked.

I want you. She bit back the words, aware that if she uttered them, the dam of restraint within her would shatter and the truths he sought would burst free.

"I asked you a question, Viva."

His terse tone of voice jerked her back to the present. "Not right now, but thank you."

"Let's get this over with, then."

She glanced at his profile as they stepped out onto the deserted balcony. She registered Spence's self-control in the muscle ticking high in his jaw and in the lines of stress that bracketed his mouth.

She missed his touch the moment that he released her arm, but she vanquished the plea that sprang to her lips. She refused to beg, refused to humiliate herself.

Instead, she watched Spence cross the deep balcony. Once he paused at the railing, she drank in the sight of him, memorizing not for the first time the lean, muscled lines of his tall body, the width of his shoulders, and the narrowness of his hips.

She remembered what it had been like to have him as a lover. Her memories weakened her knees, so she remained where she stood, fighting the desire spilling into her veins like a waterfall of scalding honey, and fighting the overwhelming need to seek shelter and safety in his embrace.

She also recalled the feelings he aroused with his hands and mouth on her naked body. Skimming. Tasting. Sucking. Tantalizing her until she'd thought she might go mad from the array of sensations that had made her quake with desire for him.

Stifling the hunger welling up inside of her as she peered at him, she also recalled the emotional sense of rightness that she'd experienced during their lovemaking. She loved this man, loved him with her entire being, even if he might never know that particular truth in his quest to discover other truths.

How could she not love him? she wondered then.

It didn't matter that he was angry with her now or that he'd been rude. She'd rejected him. For his sake, of course, but he hadn't understood her motive. She knew that it would be a very long time before she would have the chance to defend herself and her actions. Would he even want to listen? She doubted it as she gazed at him.

Shaken by her thoughts, Viva struggled with her emotions. Several long minutes passed—minutes filled with the sound of the surf crashing against the rocks below the deck—before she trusted herself enough to join Spence at the railing. Although her nerves were raw and her heart was racing, her determination remained intact.

"I'm listening," he said as they stood side by side, both white-knuckled as they gripped the railing and stared out at the encroaching darkness.

"Look at me, Spence," Viva whispered as she turned to face him. "Please look at me and stop pretending that I'm invisible."

He complied with her request, but with obvious reluctance. In his stormy gaze Viva glimpsed his anger and the hurt she'd caused. She wanted to weep for them both. She also wanted to comfort Spence. But she steeled herself against both impulses.

"You've been avoiding me," she remarked, taking the proverbial bull by the horns.

"I've been busy."

"We've both been busy."

"Are you finished?" he demanded.

"You're determined to be difficult, aren't you?"

"Am I?"

"This war of nerves needs to stop now, for both our sakes."

"Does it?"

Viva exhaled raggedly. "Why don't we declare a truce?" she suggested. "That way, we—"

"Not good enough," he informed her.

"Spence . . ."

"Not . . . good . . . enough," he said a second time, carefully enunciating each word.

Annoyed, she lost control of her temper and snapped, "I heard you the first time."

"Good. We're actually making some progress then, since you don't seem to have heard anything else I've said to you in the last three or four weeks."

"I don't deserve that from you," she told him.

"Why the hell not?"

"It doesn't matter why. It just matters that your attitude is the pits. You've already pointed out the importance of a united front in our partnership. Being openly hostile when I'm in the same building makes no sense at all."

"Think again, partner."

"That's all I've been doing for the last ten days," she confessed in a rush of words that she immediately regretted.

"Why waste the time or energy?"

"Quit with the sarcasm. Can't we put aside our differences and have a civil conversation?"

"Great idea," he shot back at her. "Shall we start with a philosophical discussion regarding the merits of honesty?"

"This is going nowhere fast," she concluded with unconcealed frustration.

Viva pushed away from the railing, but before she took her first step, Spence stopped her with a hand on her shoulder. She glared at him, but she didn't attempt to evade his restraining grip.

"Lies and secrets are like dead ends, Viva."

"I haven't lied to you."

"I think you have."

"As for secrets," she continued stubbornly, "if I am keeping secrets, that's my choice. I won't be bullied. Not by you or anyone else."

"Who is he, Viva?"

Startled and instantly wary, she looked at him. "What do you mean?"

"Who or what has you so terrified that you've stopped recognizing the difference between people who care about you and people who want things from you?"

She steadied herself with a calming breath. "The point of this conversation is to forge some kind of a truce between us."

"A truce is useless without honesty. Besides, I want a hell of a lot more from you than a truce."

Viva nodded, then forced herself to sound quite matter-of-fact. "You want my body."

"Dammit, Viva! You know I want more than sex. I want you, and I'm certain you want me."

She went very still inside. He wanted her, the woman. She wanted him, but she couldn't have him. Not now, anyway, and she still couldn't explain why.

Deal with reality, she told herself. She knew she had no other choice. "We've had this conversation before, Spence. If we have it again, the end result will be the same as the first time."

He ignored her cautionary remark. "I also want answers. I will not settle for less from you."

"Be reasonable, Spence."

"You will never meet a more reasonable man."

"Or a more stubborn one," she countered.

"At least I'm behaving in character. You, on the other hand, are not."

"I can't give you what you want!" she exclaimed.

"Why?" he demanded as he grabbed her and

jerked her against his hard frame. "Just this once, answer a direct question with a direct answer. Tell me why."

She slumped against him, momentarily undone by his demands. "Don't do this to me, Spence. Please."

"I don't have any other choice," he ground out.

"I can't," she whispered once she lifted her head and met his gaze. "I'm sorry, but I just can't."

"Viva, you're exhausted, you've lost more weight since we were together, and you're tied up in knots over something you can't or won't discuss," he itemized. "You lied to the police. You ran away from home after Michael's funeral, and you haven't been back since. You neglected Tommy, but you loved him and talked to him as often as his health permitted before he had his final heart attack." Gripping her upper arms, he gave her a little shake. "Tell me your behavior makes sense. Tell me, Viva, and then maybe I'll back off."

Stunned, she stared up at him. Tears welled in her eyes. "I'm doing what I have to do." A sob ripped through her, then another. Embarrassed by her own weakness, she sucked in a sharp breath.

Visibly alarmed, Spence gentled his hold on her. "I think you really believe what you're saying, but you're coming apart at the seams. Let me help you, little one, before you destroy yourself."

"Be my friend," she begged softly. "I need that from you. I need it more than you know. And accept the fact that we can be partners in the business, but that's all."

"I've never not been your friend. I'm trying my damnedest to be that now, but you're not making it easy for me." He scanned her features. "Look, I'm worried about you. I don't want to lose you too."

"You won't lose me as long as we're friends and partners," she assured him.

"I'm having a tough time believing you," Spence said.

A sudden movement on the far side of the balcony caught Viva's attention. Glancing beyond Spence, she saw a tall, impeccably dressed man step out onto the balcony.

Shocked, she blinked and refocused, certain that she'd finally lost her mind. The man was real, though. So real that she almost bolted in the next heartbeat. Paling, she abruptly jerked free of Spence and stumbled backward.

"Viva? What the hell's wrong now?"

She heard the sound of Spence's voice, but the words amounted to little more than a roaring in her ears. Fear clawed at her, threatening to completely destroy her composure.

On the verge of total panic, Viva smoothed a stray lock of hair away from her cheek with shaking fingers and gave Spence a strained smile. "I have to go now. I have another commitment this evening, so please don't try to stop me."

She turned away from him with an uncharacteristic lack of grace and made her way across the balcony. Riveted in place by her abruptness, Spence watched her departure in a state of disbelief.

"Good evening, Mr. Renaud," she said. Viva didn't break stride as the Cajun-born financier, a man she'd encountered several times at racetracks across the country, returned her polite greeting.

As Viva disappeared into the crowded cliffside mansion, leaving silence in her wake, Spence jerked free of his shock. The fear and panic he'd glimpsed in her eyes flashed through his mind like a blazing neon sign. He started to follow her, but he paused when he noticed the smug look on the face of Daltry Renaud, his late stepbrother's former business associate.

Spence disliked few people, but Renaud occupied star billing on that short list. He knew the man's unsavory reputation as well as any other Thoroughbred owner, but his dislike had become personal when his stepbrother had gotten involved with Renaud a few years prior to his death.

Michael had always insisted that they were nothing more than co-investors in several business transactions, although he'd consistently declined to explain the nature of those business dealings when questioned by Spence or Tommy Conrad.

Spence had once even wondered if his association with Renaud had somehow contributed to his death. His suspicion was more the result of a gut-level feeling than anything else, but he hadn't had the time after the funeral to pursue it. Viva had disappeared and Tommy's health had taken a nose-dive, leaving the responsibilities of the partnership and its extensive holdings to Spence.

Now, Spence wondered again if there was a link. He knew that Renaud operated in the shadows of the Thoroughbred world. Suspected of fixing races, buying off jockeys, and arranging the deaths of several highly insured Thoroughbreds, Renaud made a lot of people very nervous. Michael had known all that, and yet he'd still aligned himself with Renaud.

Why? Another unanswered question. Spence swore under his breath, the foul word a reflection of his frustration.

Daltry Renaud inclined his head like a king intent on being gracious to a peon. "Ah, Hammond, it's been a long time. I trust you are well, sir."

Spence jerked a nod in his direction, his thoughts shifting to Renaud's presence at Michael's funeral.

"Miss Conrad seemed in a hurry to leave. Is she ill?" Renaud inquired.

"You'd have to ask the lady," he advised, not bothering to conceal his disdain for the man.

Renaud nodded his agreement. "An excellent suggestion. I shall, of course, do that when I encounter her at the track. I gather you have high hopes for Anticipation. My sources tell me that her breezes are quite impressive."

He studied Renaud through narrowed eyes. It occurred to him then that Viva had fled the balcony within moments of seeing the man. Why? he wondered.

Some instinct he couldn't quite name urged him to explore the possibility of a connection between Viva's panicked flight in the middle of their conversation and Daltry Renaud. Was he grasping at straws? He suddenly didn't think so. The added possibility that Michael had entangled Viva in one of Renaud's questionable business schemes might help to explain her erratic behavior during the previous year, Spence reasoned.

"Mr. Hammond?"

He gave the man a hard look. "Your sources are accurate. Anticipation is doing quite well."

"I shall have to place an appropriate wager on her," Renaud commented, his accent pronounced.

Spence shrugged. "It's your money." Turning, he walked away.

"Have a pleasant evening, Mr. Hammond," the Cajun called out after him.

Spence ignored the man and his remark. He reached the circular driveway at the front of the mansion in time to see Viva slip into her car and speed down the hill. Handing his claim ticket to one of the valets, he waited impatiently for his car to be brought around.

As he guided the vehicle out of Del Mar and onto the freeway, Spence couldn't dismiss from his mind Daltry Renaud or Viva's reaction to him. He arrived at her hilltop estate thirty minutes later and discovered that Viva had forgotten to change the code on the security system.

Once he tapped out the numbers, Spence proceeded onto the property after the gate opened, glancing in the rearview mirror to make certain it rolled closed behind him before he continued up the long driveway.

He found Viva pacing in the rose garden adjacent to the main house. Spence stood in the shadows of several giant eucalyptus trees and observed her for several minutes.

His anger with her faded as he took in her agitated state. He knew then that she needed more than love or comfort from him. She needed an ally, and he vowed that he would assume that role whether or not she was willing to offer him anything other than her friendship in the future.

Spence ached inside when he saw the tears streaming down her cheeks as she walked aimlessly along the flagstone path that wove through the rose garden. Stepping out of the concealing shadows and into her path, he said, "I'm here to help you."

Viva stumbled to a stop. Before she could turn away, Spence took her hands. She exhaled, the sound filled with weariness, and her shoulders slumped with the kind of defeat that tore at Spence's heart. This woman barely resembled the Viva of old.

"You don't have to run from me anymore."

She peered up at him, her lashes spiked by her tears, her entire body trembling in spite of the balmy temperatures of the August evening. "You had no right to come here without an invitation, Spence. No right at all."

"I don't agree." He kept his tone of voice mild, his body language as unthreatening as possible, because he heard not just her frustration, but a hint of panic.

"You've got to stop hounding me."

He smiled gently. "I don't think that's what I'm doing."

"You have to stay away from me."

"I can't do that, little one, so don't even waste your breath asking me a second time, all right?"

She ignored him. "Please leave," she said, urgency underscoring the two words as she scanned the shrubs edging the rose garden before returning her gaze to him.

Spence shook his head, the negative gesture emphatic. "It's time to trust me, Viva. Will you at least try?" he asked.

He saw the battle she waged in her tormented eyes. He waited, waited for her to take the step he knew she needed to take, waited for her to finally share whatever it was that was eating her alive, and waited for her to admit that she needed his help.

Spence didn't push her. He knew better now. Something or someone had already done that to her, and the results were painfully obvious. She looked fragile, so fragile that any misstep on his part might send her running for cover yet again.

In the end, Viva didn't say a single word. She

simply nodded and walked directly into Spence's arms.

Not caring why or how this about-face had happened, Spence embraced her without hesitation. She aligned herself to him like a second skin. When he felt how slender she'd become in recent weeks, he started to grasp the extent of Viva's vulnerability.

She trembled, and he sensed that she might sink to her knees without any warning from sheer emotional and physical exhaustion. Lifting her, he cradled her against his chest, his hold on her both possessive and protective.

Once she looped her arms around his neck, he carried her out of the garden and into the main house. Spence didn't bother to turn on any lights, nor did he say anything. He held her close, his footsteps punctuating each step he took as he crossed the Italian tile entryway that led to the formal living room.

EIGHT

The wide shaft of moonlight spilling into the room provided all the illumination Spence needed as he made a path to the couch. Once he reached it, he sank down onto the cushions with Viva still cradled in his arms.

She curled into him, her tear-dampened cheek pressed to the side of his neck, her arms wrapped around his shoulders. She held on tightly, as though she might never let go.

Spence knew better, of course. She was a woman of innate courage and resilience, not a clinging vine. Viva was also fiercely independent, except on those rare occasions when she shut down inside because something or someone blindsided her.

Spence again chose to wait for Viva, instead of pressing her for answers to the questions that had haunted him for more than a year. He waited for her to find the strength that was intrinsic to her character, just as he waited for her to remember that she could depend on him and their friendship. And he waited for her to recall what they'd shared as lovers.

Holding her close, Spence skimmed his open palms up and down her back in an attempt to help her relax. He reflected not for the first time on how essential Viva had become to his future and his happiness. He'd fallen in love with her, and he no longer wanted to imagine a life without her.

"You just won't give up on me, will you?" Amazement resonated in her voice when she finally ended her silence a short while later.

Not in this life or any other, Spence realized. "Do you really want me to?"

Viva lifted her head from his shoulder and looked at him. "A part of me does, but another part . . ." Her voice trailed off as she scrubbed the tears from her cheeks with the backs of her hands.

As he watched her in the muted light, Spence remembered a shy adolescent girl with long braids and huge blue eyes, and he remembered how protective she'd always been about those she cared for. Was that what she was doing now? he speculated silently. Protecting someone she loved?

"What about the other part?" he pressed.

"You know how much I hate feeling cornered or trapped," she hedged, not really answering his question.

"That's not what I'm doing, Viva."

She glanced at him in surprise. "I didn't mean to imply that you were. It's the situation, not you." She exhaled, resignation in the gust of air. "You must think I'm having some kind of mental breakdown after the conversation we had a little while ago and the way I've been acting."

"What I think is that you don't have to fight all of your battles alone, even though that's what you appear to be doing. I want to help, but you have to let me."

"I'm tired, Spence." Her chin wobbled as her emotions resurfaced. "And more scared than I've ever been in my entire life."

Surprised by her admission, he brought his hand up and curved his palm against the side of her face. "I can see that."

She ducked free of his touch. "Don't feel sorry for me, Spencer Hammond. I'm not some helpless dimwit who can't cope with real life."

"Relax, will you?" he urged, secretly loving this reminder of her feisty nature. As far as he was concerned, it was a major improvement on the bunker mentality she'd adopted since leaving home. "You don't need to go all prickly on me. Pity's the last thing I've ever felt where you're concerned." He gave her a quick smile and dropped a kiss on the tip of her nose. "Trust me on that, all right?"

"I do trust you. I always have. As paranoid as I probably sound right now, it's other people I don't trust." She gave him a considering look. "I can't do this alone any longer, Spence. I need your help."

"It's about damn time you realized that fact, whatever the hell *this* is."

"Don't swear," she chided without missing a beat. "It makes you sound common."

He grinned at Viva. She sounded like her old self.

"You've been missed. Welcome back."

She smiled, albeit tentatively.

As he hugged her and felt the press of her breasts against his chest, his body suddenly ignited. Spence exercised ruthless control over the brush fires that exploded to life within him, but Viva's position in his lap and the sound of her voice made a joke of his efforts to contain his response to her.

She seduced him with her mere existence. The fact that she was curled against him like a cat simply enhanced his hunger for her and made him crave a repeat of the intimacy they'd already shared. He smothered the groan building inside, the control he was known for tattering around the edges as she shifted against him.

Spence couldn't help wondering why the attraction between them hadn't emerged until now. He wanted Viva with an intensity that kept building, rather than easing. He'd already endured countless sleep-disturbed nights in recent weeks thanks to his escalating desire for her, and he expected to endure many more at the rate things were going.

Although he longed to make love with her, he tamped down the desire steaming through his veins. This wasn't the time to be self-indulgent, he reminded himself, but he wondered if there would be time for them later. Time to talk about the future. Time for him to explore the sensuality that was as natural as breathing to Viva. And time simply to share their thoughts and the hours not devoted to more worldly pursuits. Time. He longed for private time with Viva.

"What are you thinking?" Viva asked, sounding calmer.

He refocused on her, then flashed a reassuring smile her way. "About lots of things, but mostly that I'm ready to listen and that you don't have to take on the world by yourself. You never did."

She studied him, her expression clouding over. "You can't overreact if I confide in you," she cautioned.

Spence frowned as he took in her anxiety. He felt certain now that what he'd viewed as her recent intransigence about discussing Michael's death had little to do with stubbornness and everything to do with fear. But fear caused by what or by whom?

"I mean it, Spence. Promise me you won't."

"I promise," he agreed, willing to say just about anything in order to get her to open up. "Who are you afraid of, Viva?"

She paled. "We'll get to that in a few minutes. Right now, we need to talk about Michael."

"He was murdered," Spence said, conviction ringing in his blunt tone.

Viva slowly nodded. "I agree with you."

"Why didn't you say so before?" He remembered then that she'd been unwilling to speak to him in the time frame between her discovery of Michael's body and her departure four days later from Kentucky. "You let people believe that he took his own life."

"I couldn't risk it, and I had no other choice," she replied, dealing with his question and the accusation that followed in one fell swoop.

Spence searched her face. What he saw in her eyes persuaded him that she spoke the truth. Something important was missing from the puzzle, though, and he intended to locate the piece she was holding back.

"Did you see Michael die, Viva? Were you a witness to what happened that night? Is that why you wouldn't speak up? Is that why you ran away?"

She shook her head. "No. I arrived at his apartment after . . ." Viva swallowed convulsively. ". . . just after he died."

Spence frowned. "You sound very certain of the timing."

"His skin was still warm when I checked for a pulse," she choked out. "I didn't want to believe he was dead, but he was."

He embraced her, sharing his strength as best as he could. He couldn't *not* ask more questions, in spite of the obvious cost to Viva, so he continued his pursuit of the truth. "Was anyone else there when you arrived? Do you know who . . ."

"No one was there. I called the police as soon as I found him."

"The suicide note . . ."

". . . was typed and unsigned. I found it, read it, and then gave it to the police." Looking away, she inhaled, then exhaled shallowly. "Michael wasn't the kind of man to kill himself, Spence. You were right about that."

"What else was I right about?" he pressed.

"That the authorities ended their investigation because I refused to cooperate and no one else came forward." She met his gaze then, although her expression appeared guarded. "And because I encouraged them to believe that Michael was despondent over our breakup."

His voice tight with tension, Spence said, "I've spent more than a year telling myself that you had a good reason for doing that. Did you?"

"The best." She fell silent then.

He studied her through narrowed eyes. "Are you going to make me ask?" he demanded, his patience finally deserting him.

"Before I tell you what you want to know, I need to be certain that you've got a very clear picture of how deeply entrenched Michael had become in Daltry Renaud's business interests."

"Whatever they were up to, I doubt that it was legal," Spence commented, then paused to be certain that he had her attention. "I spoke to Renaud after you left the party tonight."

Viva flinched, fear flashing in her blue eyes as she peered back at Spence, unconcealed fear that he couldn't ignore.

"You spoke with him?" she said.

He shrugged, the casual gesture as misleading as his next remark. Not at all surprised that his mention of Daltry Renaud had set off alarms in Viva, he now wanted to know why. "We chatted."

"Did he say anything odd to you? Ask you any questions about me or our relationship? Make any veiled threats?"

Threats? "Of course not," he answered.

She sagged against him.

He tightened his grip on her waist without realizing it. "Talk to me, Viva. You're keeping secrets again."

"Please, Spence, let me do this in my own way."

Despite the frustration he felt, he nodded.

Viva continued, "I never understood Michael's decision to form a partnership with Renaud, but whenever I questioned him about it, he insisted that he was doing what he wanted to do and that I shouldn't interfere. When I first found out, though, I couldn't believe it. Renaud's reputation has always been terrible. You know as well as I do what he's been suspected of over the years. Insurance scams, racketeering, drugs." Pausing, she pressed her palms together. "He's done worse, though. Much worse."

"Is that why you broke your engagement to Michael?" he asked. "Because he wouldn't end his association with Renaud?"

She flushed and looked away. "No. My reasons were personal."

"Michael's decision to align himself with Renaud shocked me," Spence admitted. "And no amount of talking could persuade him to call a halt to the partnership. He was determined to go forward with Renaud, even after Tommy and I invited him to join a new investment group we were putting together. I was stunned when he said he wasn't interested. I figured we'd waited too long to include him, but the timing needed to be just right or the other investors wouldn't have accepted Michael as an equal partner. He had a reputation for recklessness as an investor."

"A deserved reputation, so don't blame yourself," Viva advised. "There wasn't anything you could have done to change his mind, but Michael said he appreciated your invitation to join the consortium."

Relief flooded him. "Did he tell you that?"

"Those were his exact words. He loved and respected you, Spence. You were his big brother, and your relationship meant a great deal to him," she confirmed.

"He always seemed to resent the way people compared him to me. He once told me that he had no intention of standing in my shadow forever."

"Other people annoyed him, Spence. You didn't. He did not get involved with Renaud to spite you, so don't even think it, all right?" Viva said emphatically.

"I'd like to think you're right."

"I am, so trust me."

He smiled. "I do."

"And I trust you," she said with a gentle answering smile, then redirected their conversation back to the path she'd initiated. "I watched Michael encourage Renaud to use his social connections, although I thought it was kind of odd. Michael actually seemed amused by the man's fascination with certain social and money circles. Circles that would never have welcomed him if it hadn't been for Michael." Viva added, "Renaud had, and probably still has, a diverse list of partners for his various business enterprises. Underworld figures from New York, some men from a Caribbean country, and a Japanese industrialist. Michael took me to several of Renaud's private parties while we were still engaged, which is how I met some of those people."

"I'm surprised he involved you in his dealings with Renaud."

"I declined after a while because I felt uncomfortable. Michael said he understood and that it was better not to tempt fate any longer. But by then he'd become a key player in Renaud's organization, so attendance wasn't really optional for him. I doubt he could have avoided those parties, or safely walked away from Renaud, even if he'd wanted to."

"Safely?" Spence repeated. "Interesting word."

"Relevant word," Viva whispered.

Spence studied her. "Where are you headed with this? I really don't need a primer on Daltry Renaud. I already know the man's a lowlife."

"I didn't want anything to happen to you and Emily," she burst out.

He went very still inside. "Why would anything happen to us? Emily's never met him, and I've never had anything but minimal contact with the man."

"You must be very careful with Renaud. He's dangerous and vengeful," she cautioned.

"I don't think he'll want to deal with me, Viva, so put your mind at rest on the subject of Daltry Renaud. He's not a threat to me, and he never will be."

Still seated in his lap, she reacted to his dismissive attitude when she gripped his shoulders. "You don't know what you're saying."

"Then spell it out," he insisted, his voice like a slab of unforgiving granite.

"Renaud is deadly, and I'm afraid of what might happen if you cross him or challenge him."

I don't have any other choice. Spence suddenly recalled Viva's words. She'd made that statement, or some variation on it, more than once in the last month when he'd questioned her behavior. "He's the reason you left Kentucky, isn't he?"

She hesitated, then nodded. "He's part of the reason."

"I saw your reaction to him tonight. Has he threatened you?"

"Not directly. At least, not yet." Slipping her arms around his waist, she shifted against him. He drew her closer, and she trembled. "You're at risk,

Spence, not me. Renaud thinks of me as a cheap form of life insurance."

Spence eased her back into view. "Life insurance?"

She trembled as she looked at him, but she maintained control over her emotions. "You must believe me when I tell you that you and Emily really are in grave danger. You have been since the night Michael died. I've spent every single day of the last fourteen months doing my very best to keep Renaud's attention away from you and Emily. The situation started unraveling when Uncle Tommy died and you arrived for the Del Mar meet. Spence, the only reason I'm telling you any of this is so that you can protect yourself. Renaud truly is a threat, and you must treat him like the viper he is."

"What makes you think you haven't misread the situation?"

"I don't think it, Spence. I know it," she insisted heatedly.

"Why, Viva? And how?" When she hesitated, he ordered, "Tell me, dammit!"

Stiffening, she glared at him.

"Please tell me," he said more quietly.

"The phone rang a few minutes after I found Michael. It was Renaud. We also spoke at the cemetery following the funeral services. Renaud told me, in very succinct terms, that your continued longevity and Emily's future depended upon my silence about Michael's relationship with him. He refused to listen to me when I told him that I didn't know anything."

"That sorry son of a—"

Viva pressed her fingertips to his lips to quiet him. "Please don't. It won't accomplish anything."

Spence didn't agree, but he consciously harnessed his rage for her sake.

"I heard from him again a few weeks ago, after we were seen together at the Del Mar track. He reminded me of our previous conversations and cautioned me that if I didn't keep my distance from you, he'd take matters into his own hands. He suggested that I leave San Diego, but I refused. Then he proposed that I sign over my inheritance to him so that you and he would be partners. You can imagine my reaction to that idea."

Spence smiled. "I'm sure you've surprised Renaud more than once."

Viva shrugged. "Maybe, I don't really know. Daltry Renaud is a street fighter. He fights dirty if he has to. The man hasn't got a conscience. He probably doesn't even know the definition of the word, now that I think about it. His bottom line is simple: There isn't anything he won't do to protect himself and the empire he's built."

His smile turned cold. The look on his face said that Renaud had met his match, even if the Cajun hadn't realized it yet.

"Don't even think about going after him," she urged. "I've seen some of the thugs he employs, and they make my blood run cold."

Spence didn't respond to her advice. Instead, he said, "Renaud blackmailed you into leaving Kentucky, Viva. I have to assume that Tommy knew what was going on, since you're living in one of his homes."

She nodded. "He helped me, and he promised to keep my whereabouts a secret from you and Emily. His death and the terms of his will changed everything, though."

"I don't like what I'm hearing, Viva. I don't like it at all. You deliberately shut me out. Why?" Spence paused and searched her features.

Viva gave him a helpless look. "I had no other choice."

"You had a choice. At least Tommy had the good sense to set things up so that I'd find you. He knew he couldn't intervene because of his failing health, but he assumed I would after he died."

"That's the conclusion I've come to," Viva admitted.

"I still can't believe you exiled yourself because of Renaud."

"You aren't being fair," she protested. "I couldn't lose you and Emily too." Scrambling out of his lap, she started to pace. "If you don't understand that, then you don't understand anything, and this entire conversation is pointless."

"Why in God's name didn't you tell me or go to the authorities?" he persisted.

She didn't break stride. "I couldn't risk Renaud finding out, and I wasn't about to tell you and have you go chasing after the man, which is exactly what you would have done. Heavens! You still might," she fretted.

"He killed Michael, didn't he?"

His question stopped her in her tracks. Looking at him, she wrapped her arms around her waist. "He as much as admitted that he'd ordered Michael's death when I spoke to him after the funeral, but I don't know why. I didn't want to make him angry, so I didn't pursue it. I came to the conclusion that if I just faded into the woodwork, then he'd leave you and Emily alone. He called me his insurance policy. It worked until Uncle Tommy died, but now you're both in danger again."

Spence pushed to his feet and walked to the wall of windows. He paused there and stared out into the darkness.

Viva followed him, positioning herself beside him. "You must protect yourself and Emily until Renaud can be stopped."

"Is he having you watched?" Spence asked, finally turning to look at her.

"Somewhat sporadically, from what I can tell."

"The way you've been acting is finally starting to make some sense, but I still don't understand why you didn't confide in me when this mess first began."

"I was afraid to risk it."

"I'd like about five minutes alone with that bastard," he exploded angrily. "Just five minutes."

She reached out and placed her hand on his

arm. "Please don't, Spence. Renaud is the one who belongs in jail, not you. The only reason I've told you any of this is so that you can protect yourself. If you confront Renaud, you and Emily are liable to wind up like Michael. I can't . . . I couldn't—" She abruptly stopped speaking in order to regain her composure. "I'm not prepared to lose the two of you. Tommy and Michael are gone, and that's enough loss to endure. I cannot handle any more."

Spence fell silent as he pondered the expression on Viva's face and mulled over her choice of words. He knew that she'd left something out. Something critical to the overall situation and to them personally, he sensed. "Why did you end your engagement to Michael?"

Obviously startled by his question, she opened her mouth to speak, then snapped it shut in the next second. Spence didn't miss the way her surprise turned into wariness as she took a moment to formulate her response.

"I told you before, I couldn't give Michael what he deserved."

"Which was?"

"Love," she whispered. "I wasn't in love with him, although I did love him."

"Was there someone else?"

."Spence, this is hardly the time to go into all that. Why don't we stay focused on Renaud? He's the biggest hazard on the horizon at present."

"We're going to have to talk about it," he warned.

"But not now," she said stubbornly. Viva slipped away from him, made her way across the room, and then pivoted gracefully to look back at him. "Would you like a drink or something to eat while we figure out what we're going to do?"

"Trying to hostess me into submission?" He smiled as he strolled to where she stood.

She bristled, but she stayed put even though he towered over her. "I was just being polite."

He shook his head. "No, you weren't. You were deliberately avoiding a direct question. It's the most annoying habit you've acquired since you left home."

"When I want a personality critique, I'll hire a professional," she said, her tension flaring. "Now, would you like a cognac or not?"

He grinned at her.

"Have you lost your mind? We have a crisis on our hands, and we have to decide on a course of action."

He shrugged. "I just can't help thinking that if we're going to stop Renaud, then the truth between us is critical. Isn't it?"

"Of course. I haven't lied to you about the risk he poses or about my belief that he's responsible for Michael's death, even if he didn't pull the trigger himself. You know everything I know."

"Do I?" he asked.

She stared up at him as he brought his hand to her face and then skimmed his fingertips down the side of her cheek. Viva glanced away, but not before Spence noticed the color staining her normally fair complexion.

"Spence . . . ," she began once she refocused on him.

He placed both hands on her shoulders, nudged her forward until she connected with his muscular body, then smoothed his palms downward from her shoulders to her hips. She flowed into him with a sigh. His heart swelled with relief.

The lush curves and hollows of her figure, combined with her unique fragrance, filled him with sensory awareness and caused incendiary little bursts of response in his bloodstream that reminded him of summer lightning in the Kentucky hill country. Spence shuddered, his breath rushing out of him as he embraced her more securely.

Viva slipped her arms around his waist. He felt what remained of her resistance drain out of her in the moments that followed.

"What are we going to do about Renaud?" she finally asked.

"We're going to bring him down, of course."

She studied his hard-angled face. "How?"

"With the right kind of help."

Lowering his head, he claimed her lips in a gentle kiss. She moaned, the sound equal parts protest and disbelief. Then she came alive as all the repressed feelings inside of her broke free of their moorings. He drank in the erotic sound, savoring her responsiveness as she angled her head and parted her lips. Too hungry for her to contain himself, he embraced both the woman and her passionate nature.

Their desire for each other blazed to life like a comet burning a path across a night sky. It tempted. It seduced. And it even made them forget, if only for a brief time, that they were about to do battle with a killer.

They touched and stroked each other, the barrier of their clothing soon an unwanted impediment as they began to address the need that had built during their time apart. They parted just long enough to hurriedly shed their clothing.

Dropping to his knees in front of Viva, Spence skimmed her silk hose down her legs and tossed them aside. Next he freed the clasp at the front of her bra, brushed it out of his way, and filled his hands with the firm globes.

She shivered, his name spilling past her lips. Her back arched as she gripped his wide shoulders. Leaning forward, he sucked the tip of one breast into his mouth while caressing the other with his fingers. He used his teeth on the taut nipple, then swirled his tongue in a circular pattern that sent streaks of flame the length of her trembling body.

He suckled her until her knees threatened to buckle, but he offered her no respite from his sensual assault. While he moved back and forth between her breasts with an insatiable appetite, he also swept his fingertips up the insides of her thighs until she shook like a willow subjected to gusting winds. Then he carefully explored the heart of her

femininity. She gasped his name, and she swayed
unsteadily. He ended his erotic torture, surged to
his feet, and swung her up and into his arms.

He carried her across the moon-washed living
room, his gaze locked on the face of the seductive
woman who had captured his heart. He turned her
so that she faced him, then smoothed her legs
around his narrow hips. She circled his shoulders
with her arms. Her breasts plumped invitingly
against his hard chest, her nipples like tight little
knots. Once he reached their destination, he lowered himself into a seated position on the couch
that faced the wall of windows.

Neither one even noticed the panoramic view
of twinkling lights atop the buildings of the city.
They saw only each other.

The world faded away, as did the worrisome
people who populated it. They felt only what lovers
feel, their senses so vibrant and attuned to the emotions flowing between them that nothing possessed
the power to interest them.

As she straddled Spence's muscular thighs, Viva
smiled at him. He again filled his hands with her
breasts and tugged at the distended tips. Sensation
sizzled in her bloodstream. She made a purring
sound.

"Feel good?" he asked, his seductive tone
heightening the sensuality of the moment.

"Better than good," she answered, sounding
breathless.

Her gaze on his face, Viva reached down to the

aroused flesh trapped between their bodies, shifted backward a few inches, and freed his pulsing strength. She clasped him, the length and thickness of him filling her hands. He jerked beneath her touch, then ground his teeth together as she lightly stroked him.

She caressed him while he unconsciously held his breath. He felt the pressure of her fingertips intensify slightly with each upward motion of her hands. When he groaned, she smiled. He released a ragged breath, his hands closing snugly over her full breasts.

"Be careful," he cautioned through gritted teeth as she teased and tantalized him.

"I love touching you. I also love it when you touch me."

He smiled, but it was a strained smile. "I need you, little one."

"Then take me," she invited.

"What do you want?" he asked.

"You."

He leaned forward and captured her mouth, plundering it so thoroughly that she was shaking when he pulled back. "How do you want me?"

She edged closer as she brought her hands up to frame his face. His sex, caught now against the moist folds of flesh at the apex of her thighs, throbbed. "Inside me?" she said boldly.

"That's where I want to be." He bracketed her hips between his hands to stop her squirming.

"What are we waiting for?" Viva asked as she tried without success to scoot forward.

He stopped her. "An answer."

She leaned back a little, looking confused. "Ask a question, then."

"I already did."

Despite the strain evident in the angular lines of his face and the tension tightening the muscles of his entire body, Spence waited. He waited for her to understand what he was asking. It took just a few seconds.

"I'm surprised at you," she chided.

"No, you're not," he disagreed.

"Of course, I am." She promptly reversed herself. "On second thought, I'm not."

"Good."

She gave him a belligerent look. "You want the truth? Fine, here's the truth. I fell in love with someone when Michael and I were engaged. I didn't expect it to happen, but it did. The rest is history."

"Do I know him?"

"That's another question," she pointed out.

"I deserve an answer. If I don't get one, then I'm going to draw a conclusion I don't think you want me to draw."

"Yes," she said softly. "You know him."

"Keep talking."

"Why?" she asked, her stubborn streak emerging.

He arched an eyebrow, but he didn't say a word.

"You're embarrassing me."

He kept his eyes on her face as he lifted her and shifted her forward. She caught her breath in surprise. He held her poised above his maleness, close enough to feel the heat of his skin but far enough away to keep her from shifting her hips and impaling herself.

Uttering a sound of complete exasperation, Viva dug her fingers into his shoulders. He simply looked at her, his face still empty of expression.

"I fell in love with you, Spencer Hammond. Are you satisfied now?" Viva demanded.

NINE

"I might be satisfied in about fifty years," Spence muttered in a desire-roughened voice.

Because Viva was still perched atop his thighs, he clasped her around the waist and lifted her as he simultaneously pushed up to his feet. He executed a half-turn, then toppled her backward onto the couch. She landed in a very startled and very naked sprawl atop the cushions.

He came down over her, his body weight braced by his arms as he settled his hips between her thighs. Although he longed to join their bodies in the ultimate intimacy, he refrained from entering her. Instead he met her gaze as she stared up at him.

"You don't seem at all surprised," she managed, her tone faintly accusatory.

"I'm not," he answered, when in truth he was stunned. He was also more relieved than he could even begin to express, so he didn't waste time searching for the words to describe the state of his emotions. That would come later, he promised himself. But for now, he needed to be physically connected to Viva. He needed the spontaneity of her passion, and the sensuality that was integral to her personality.

As he looked at her, primitive urges flowed through his consciousness and his body. He gathered her into his arms, immediately feeling the tremors shimmying through her torso and the hard-nippled bounty of her full breasts as they plumped against the wall of his muscular chest.

He shuddered, his eyes falling closed as he threw back his head and ground his teeth together. Somehow, he maintained rigid control over himself. He wanted and needed Viva, the compelling urge to validate her admission of love close to devastating what had already been reduced to very questionable control on his part.

"Did you suspect the truth all along?" she asked as another shiver of awareness moved through her body. She gripped his shoulders as she waited for him to answer her question.

Words were impossible, so Spence didn't even try. When he felt the kneading pressure of her fingertips move across his shoulders and then up the sides of his neck, the tension lodged deep inside him grew dangerously acute. He exhaled, the sound ragged as he warred with the primal instinct to mate.

"I need you." She tugged his head down and nibbled at his lower lip ever so carefully. "I need to feel you inside of me, Spence. Now."

The thunderous beating of his heart deafened him. His control vanished in the next split second. He drove into her silken depths, claiming her for himself and for the balance of eternity. He groaned as he sank into the tight, wet heat of her body, certain that he would never be able to let her go now that he knew that she loved him.

She gasped his name as he buried himself to the hilt, then she arched upward in response to the surging force of his engorged maleness. He pumped into her, unable to restrain his need and unwilling to delay his possession of her. As far as he was concerned, too much time had already been wasted.

Tangling her fingers at his nape, Viva responded to his claiming as though suddenly subjected to a thousand volts of pure energy. She writhed against Spence with an openly erotic display of her desire for him.

He trembled when he felt the delicate flesh of her inner body clutch at his manhood. He fought again for control, while his relief at knowing the truth and too many days and nights of pent-up desire finally blended to form a searing current of sensation that traveled like wildfire throughout his body.

Just seconds later he remembered something he didn't really want to remember—his anxiety that he still might lose Viva when this night ended and they faced the dawn once again. In order to banish the negative thought, he took her lips and thrust his tongue into her mouth in an aggressive imitation of the movement of his lower torso. He deliberately used his body to convey the emotions threatening to swamp him, his need to claim the woman he knew he would love until he drew his last breath dominating his consciousness.

She undulated beneath him as he repeatedly speared into her, partially withdrew, and then plunged even more deeply into the tight channel of her body. The gasping little sounds she made spurred him on, as did the feelings caused by her fingernails lightly scoring his skin as she gripped his hips with both hands.

Viva trembled violently in response to the far-reaching physical and emotional reverberations of Spence's possession. The perfect lover, he made her feel as though she was the center of his universe and the sole reason for his existence as their passion consumed them and made them one.

Clinging to him, she basked in the sensations spiraling through her body. Their pace escalated to a level of intensity that surpassed anything she'd ever before experienced with a man. She gave all that she possessed in the minutes that followed, her emotions released from the bondage of restraint and silence forced upon her since her departure from Kentucky.

As they moved in swift, fluid harmony, Viva experienced a tightening inside, a coiling kind of feeling that suffused her body with a rainbow of glittering sensations. A sudden sense of urgency overwhelmed her, scattering her thoughts until nothing mattered other than finding fruition with Spence.

As though sensing her need, he quickened his pace even more. She reacted instinctively to him, finding unexpected validation in the intrinsic beauty of life, emotional sustenance, and the certainty that Spence was the mate intended for her as their lover's ballet turned frenzied and frantic. Her heart seemed on the verge of flying free of her body.

When she suddenly wrenched her mouth free, threw her head back, and cried out his name, Spence covered her breasts with his hands, lowered his lips to her exposed throat, and sharpened his angle of penetration. Their bodies merged over and over again with barely contained violence, achieving a oneness unique to lovers mating physically, emotionally, and spiritually.

Viva moaned out his name when she started to unravel inside. Her climax detonated across her senses like a fireball. She stiffened briefly, then surrendered to the torrent of sensations sweeping over and through her.

Spence skillfully prolonged her release by gentling his deep strokes. His efforts to satisfy Viva produced a stunned cry of disbelief and pleasure from her. He followed her into the glittering oblivion just moments later, his control shattered by the rhythmic sucking sensation of her quivering body and the words of love she uttered as she reached the zenith of her release.

He climaxed explosively. Wave after wave of sensation rolled through him, wreaking the sweetest kind of sensual havoc possible.

Spent and still shaking a short while later, he drew Viva with him as he rolled onto his side. They collapsed in a tangle of sweat-drenched limbs, both struggling for air and both thoroughly weakened by the releases they'd just shared.

Their bodies still intimately joined, Spence cradled Viva against his chest as their respiration slowly returned to normal. Tiny tremors, like aftershocks, continued to move through Viva, and he felt even the subtlest of the quakes each time her body squeezed like a fist around his maleness.

Although understandably drained of energy, Spence also felt strangely exhilarated. His desire for Viva started to renew itself as she shifted against him, trailed a string of little kisses along his collarbone, and then stroked him from shoulder to hip. The respite he'd anticipated she would need failed to materialize in the moments that followed.

Viva nudged him onto his back. She flowed along with him so that their bodies remained connected. Crouched astride Spence, she whispered kisses all over his face before shifting her lips to his.

He clasped her hips between his hands when he felt the internal muscles of her body tremor around him. He groaned low in his throat, the sound inspiring her to deepen what had begun as a light, playful kiss.

She darted her tongue into the heat of his mouth and instigated a sensual duel that sent streaks of desire across the horizon of his senses. Her hands seemed to be everywhere at once, stroking fingertips, skimming palms, fingernails dragged ever so carefully over his nugget-hard nipples.

She teased. She tantalized. She reawakened. And, he realized, she deliberately set out to seduce him until she made him ache with a depth of hunger that defied explanation. She was well on her way to success in a very short time.

Spence welcomed her aggression, and he embraced her erotic sensitivities. He'd never known a woman like Viva. She was his siren. He savored the knowledge that she was this way only with him and because of her love for him.

As she continued to caress him, more and more intimately with each stroke of her fingertips, heat pooled low in his belly and then flooded his loins. His pulse quickened. His blood felt hot and sluggish, his skin seemed on the verge of being scorched, and his maleness throbbed with life and the need for yet another release. He marveled once more over her evocative nature, and he gloried in his role as the beneficiary of the instincts that guided her.

Viva lifted her hips a few inches and then sank down over him again as she teased and toyed with his tongue. She moved once more, this time adding a subtle twist to her hip movement halfway down his engorged shaft.

Spence sucked in a harsh breath, then another as she repeated the action a third time. Viva sighed into his mouth. He drank in the sound.

Drawing back slightly, she smiled at him. "Hi."

"Hi, yourself."

She kept swaying, her bent legs giving her the leverage she needed to continue her movement. He covered her full breasts with his hands, then tugged at the nipples until they tightened into hard little knots. He twisted them carefully, eliciting a low moan of pleasure from Viva as her head lolled to the side and her eyes fell closed.

She dipped and swayed as he caressed her. Spence felt as though he was viewing an erotic dance created for his pleasure alone. He closed his eyes, awash in sensation as his hardness grew slick with the essence of her femininity. Too aroused now to deny himself, he reared up from the couch and cupped her swollen breasts.

He shifted back and forth between her nipples, alternately sucking and lightly biting the sensitive flesh until she trembled and moaned. The feelings he evoked prompted her to settle even more firmly atop his hips, thus impaling herself as completely as possible with his pulsating sex.

"Talk to me," Spence said raggedly, palming the full globes and tugging at the taut peaks once he sank back against the cushions again.

She opened her eyes to peer down at him. "I don't . . . think I . . . can."

"You sound out of breath." He stroked her from the tight mauve tips down to the nest of silky dark hair at the base of her abdomen, then back up again, his fingertips sending shivers of sensation through her.

She gasped softly. "It's your fault."

Smiling, he urged her forward with the lightest pressure of his fingertips at her shoulders. With the kind of grace that was as natural to her as breathing, Viva accepted his cue, folded forward at the waist, and flowed over him.

After slipping her arms around him, she turned her face into the hard curve that joined his shoulder and neck, nuzzling him with her lips, then shifted to press a kiss against the hollow at the base of his throat. She tongued the pulse hammering there at her leisure before she lifted her head and met his gaze.

"I'm on fire for you again," Spence said as he framed her face with hands that shook.

"Is that bad?" she asked.

He chuckled at her playfulness. "Unexpected."

"You thought you'd be bored with me after one time?"

"Right," he said. "I'm bored to tears. I've also got a bridge and an island for sale."

She laughed, unknowingly giving him a glimpse of their long-standing friendship and some of the special moments they'd shared in the past. "I'm happy."

Her laughter and the announcement she'd just made reminded Spence that she hadn't been really happy in a very long time. He silently promised himself that she would be once their lives returned to normal. "Why didn't you give me some kind of a hint about your feelings before you left?"

Her smile disappeared. Slowly straightening, she asked, "What purpose would it have served, Spence?"

He didn't know quite how to answer her as he watched the sparkle leave her eyes. She pressed her fingertips to the bridge of her nose, as though to massage away pain.

Viva finally lowered her hand and looked at him. "I didn't want to hurt Michael. Nor did I want to make you uncomfortable or embarrass you, much less strain a friendship that was very important to me, so I did the best I could given the situation. I ended the engagement without telling Michael anything about my feelings for you, and then I tried to move forward with my life, but his death and Renaud's part in it, plus the way he blackmailed me, changed everything. You know the rest, and I suspect that you would have done the same thing if you'd have been in my shoes."

"I wondered if you'd told Michael," Spence admitted, his expression troubled.

He already knew that his stepbrother had spent much of his life battling the comparisons people felt compelled to make between the two Hammond offspring. Losing the woman he loved to his older brother could have done irreparable damage, but Viva hadn't allowed that to happen. Spence drew a small measure of comfort from the fact that Viva had safeguarded their relationship, but she'd paid a high price for her protectiveness. He owed her a great deal for that, and for many other things, he realized.

Her expression reflective, conviction rang in her voice as she remarked, "Telling Michael the entire truth wouldn't have been right."

He clasped her upper arms and drew her forward when she shivered, this time from the breeze moving into the room through the open patio doors. Viva wound up in a sexy sprawl atop him, their loins still mated despite the unexpected direction of their conversation.

"We're *right* now, though," he said as he stroked his hands from her hips to her waist and then up to her shoulders before he reversed course. He couldn't not touch Viva. "We're very right, little one."

She smiled, but not with the high-wattage brilliance he'd hoped for. Spence noticed a hint of melancholy in her expression. He hugged her, the need to reassure himself that she was real, and his, coming out of nowhere and startling him with its intensity. Her silence persisted even when he eased his hold on her.

"You're awfully quiet. Don't you agree that we're right for each other?" he asked.

Viva nodded. "I think so."

"You *think* so?"

"I've learned not to expect too much, Spence. It hurts too badly when things don't work out."

"*We* will work out," he insisted, his embrace tightening.

Slipping free of his hold, she announced, "I don't want to speculate about the past or the future. In fact, living in the moment really appeals to me right now, although I've always considered people who do it somewhat shortsighted. All I want to do is touch and be touched. I want to spend hours devoted exclusively to feeling, and then I want you to hold me while we sleep." She smoothed a fingertip across the width of his lower lip, then back again. "Beyond that . . ."

When she abruptly paused, he saw the tears that filled her eyes before she blinked them away. Then she lifted her chin in a gesture of determination that Spence recognized, although it broke his heart to see it.

". . . Beyond that," Viva continued after she cleared her throat, "I won't let myself want too much. I can't. At least not until Renaud isn't a threat to you and Emily."

Spence made an effort not to overreact to Viva's renewed worry. He spanned her narrow waist with his hands, silently mourning the fact that she felt the need to remain so guarded, but he understood the reasons for her caution. She'd been summarily robbed of her illusions, not just her home, her loved ones, and her identity. It would take her time to feel in control of her life again, he realized.

She sighed, then managed a lopsided smile. "I think you're looking at a woman who wants the night off from reality."

Spence nodded. "I'm looking at a woman who deserves to have anything she wants."

She promptly stage-whispered, "I want you."

He smiled at her. "And how would you like me?" Spence asked, sounding equally conspiratorial.

She paused, as if to consider a weighty question that had the potential of altering the course of human events. The network of delicate muscles deep in her body tremored suddenly around the length and thickness of his manhood, which was still firmly lodged inside her. She flashed a startled look at Spence.

He cursed, the word emerging like a hiss of shock, then said, "Hell of an answer!" His voice sounded as rough as a stretch of torn-up road, which made perfect sense to him since that was how he felt at the moment. Torn up.

"I think I'll demonstrate, instead." Viva leaned forward and placed her hands, both palms down, on his shoulders while simultaneously rocking her hips from side to side.

Spence bit back a moan. "I take it we're making this up as we go along?"

"We can do anything we want to do."

"As long as we do it together," he finished for her.

He clasped her hips, but he didn't try to still her movement. Using his hands like brackets, he absorbed the seductive rhythm of her undulating body with his palms while friction arced up and down another part of his anatomy. His eyes fell closed, and a ragged breath spilled past his lips. "You amaze me," he muttered.

"Why?" She gripped his shoulders as she crouched over him, the tension inside of her steadily increasing. Flushed and obviously aroused, she closed her eyes and rode the storm-induced tide building within even as she rode Spence.

He abandoned his restraint just seconds later. Thrusting upward, he savored the glovelike tightness of Viva's body. He managed to groan through gritted teeth, "Because you're amazing."

Viva nipped at his chin, then breathlessly confided, "I'm a little amazed myself. I've never felt quite so . . . uninhibited."

"Good, because we won't be having any inhibitions, barriers, or boundaries between us. Not ever."

"If that's what you want, then that's exactly what you'll get," Viva promised.

She kept her promise throughout the night. By the time she surrendered to physical exhaustion, the dawn had unfolded across the clear August morning sky and Spence had repeatedly claimed her heart and her body.

He also staked a silent but permanent claim on Viva's future within the privacy of his heart, even though he doubted that she realized it. He refrained from saying anything to her about the life he wanted them to share. Their current situation was tenuous enough, he knew, but he allowed himself optimism.

It was early Sunday afternoon before they roused themselves from their bed, showered, dressed, and went in search of nourishment. Joining forces in the kitchen, Viva and Spence prepared a platter of deli-style sandwiches and an array of tasty side dishes, found the perfect bottle of wine, and then carried everything outside on trays to one of the patio tables.

They lingered over their meal on the sun-washed deck that overlooked the bay, chatting about inconsequential matters until they finished eating. After Spence refilled their wineglasses, they finally talked about how to end Daltry Renaud's stranglehold on their lives.

"Any good ideas?" Viva asked as she sank back in her chair and studied Spence.

"The only thing that makes sense is to approach the federal authorities," he said without hesitation. "This guy has an army to back him up, and we'd be fools to take him on ourselves."

"Wasn't he under investigation a few years ago by the Justice Department?" she asked.

Spence nodded. "He was suspected of extortion and money laundering, but I don't think he was ever charged. He's a known quantity with the feds, though, and that fact alone probably guarantees that they'll at least listen."

"They may not take us seriously," she remarked as she reached for her sunglasses and perched them on her face.

"That's a risk I'm going to take, Viva."

She gave him a questioning look. He met her gaze, his own a study in implacability, and she realized what he meant. "We're going to do this together."

He shook his head. "Not a good idea. I'll take the lead until we establish some ground rules with the authorities. Drawing Renaud's attention to you is the last thing I want to do, especially if he's having you watched."

"Forget it, Spence. We're a team. Otherwise, I won't say another word to you or anyone else."

"Be reasonable—"

"You're wasting your breath," she cut in.

"I can't believe you're serious."

"Of course, I'm serious. I've had my life turned upside down by Daltry Renaud. I'm done being made to feel like a helpless pawn." She paused, considered how her next remark might sound to Spence, then said the words anyway. "I will not forgive you if you go behind my back on this."

"You're in danger," Spence reminded her.

"Putting you under a spotlight could get you killed."

Spotlight? How odd, she thought, that he would select that particular word, especially since she'd used the same one during her conversation with Renaud, although in a different context. She knew that Spence was right about the risks involved, but Viva still intended to be with him every step of the way until the situation with Renaud was brought to some sort of a rational conclusion.

She loathed the limbo she lived in, and she wanted an end to it. She wanted her life and her freedom restored. And she wanted to be able to go home.

Viva refocused on Spence. "Despite what you think, I'm not being reckless or foolish. I'm just not willing to stand back and watch you take all the risks. We deal with Renaud as a team. It's the only way I'm willing to do this, and I'm not going to debate my decision with you."

His gaze narrowed, he finally nodded with obvious reluctance. "I keep forgetting how stubborn you can be."

She smiled. "Thank you."

Spence drained his wine, placed the goblet on the table, and got to his feet. "I need to make a call."

"Do you still carry a cellular phone with you?" she asked.

"Fine minds think alike."

She cocked her head, her expression wry. "Or

we've both watched too many suspense movies on the late, late show."

"How about a meeting at your office, if I can arrange it?" he asked.

"You might want to tell our visitors to identify themselves as pharmaceutical company reps who have appointments scheduled with me. We can use the conference room during the lunch hour," she suggested.

Spence scanned her features, then turned on his heel. As she watched Spence stride across the deck and into the house, Viva's attention shifted to purely sensual thoughts. She adored the leashed strength contained in his lean, muscled body. She'd experienced his power all through the night, as well as his gentleness.

He'd delighted her with his thoroughness as a lover, teaching her things she'd secretly wondered about and providing her with the kind of emotional security that allowed her to unleash her inhibitions. She'd felt a sense of liberation during their love-making, and a sense of emotional harmony that surpassed anything she'd ever imagined could take place between a man and a woman.

He'd amused her with moments of unexpected humor in the midst of scintillating passion. And he'd made love to her and with her, sometimes so slowly that she wanted to scream, other times with such urgent force that she thought she might disintegrate, so often during the night that she'd felt on the verge of meltdown.

But was he in love with her? she wondered, or was she making that emotional journey alone? She hoped not, although she didn't honestly know.

Viva felt the penetrating warmth of the sun as she sat on the deck, but chill bumps danced across her skin while she grappled with the reality that Spence hadn't articulated his feelings for her. She, of course, hadn't asked. And she wouldn't. Her pride wouldn't allow her to, but didn't he know that about her?

TEN

Spence spent the next twenty-four hours negotiating, via a series of telephone conversations, his terms for a meeting with investigative personnel from the Justice Department. He deliberately took advantage of the shocked pleasure he heard in the voice of the agent who took his first call, primarily because of his worry over Viva's safety. He didn't reveal his concern to her when she questioned what turned into a two-day delay before the meeting actually took place. Instead, he reminded her that they were dealing with a government bureaucracy.

Viva and Spence waited until the three men were ensconced in the conference room at the pediatric clinic during the lunch hour before making their appearance. As she made her way across the room, Viva noticed that each man wore a name tag with a pharmacy company logo. The three remained standing while Spence drew out her chair, made sure she was settled comfortably in it, and then took a seat beside her.

"Thank you for joining us," Spence began as he surveyed their faces. His gaze dipped to the identification badges they each wore. "Are those your real names or are we improvising?"

"Mr. Hammond, there isn't anything even vaguely improvisational about this meeting. You made certain of that, sir."

Viva lifted her hand in time to hide the smile caused by the man's irritated tone. She studied the speaker, a nondescript thirtyish fellow in a beige suit and mud-colored tie, and then frowned. "Although I know we haven't ever been introduced, I've seen you before."

"I doubt that, Miss Conrad."

Nerved up enough by the need for a clandestine meeting with Justice Department investigators, she stiffened in response to his dismissive attitude.

Spence stabbed the man with a hard look. "I've never made the mistake of underestimating this lady. You'd be well advised not to, either."

"Mr. Hammond, shall we get to the purpose of this meeting?" he demanded.

Viva ignored his rude prompt. "A restaurant in Los Angeles," she said, her expression thoughtful. "No, it was Marina Del Rey. Probably two years ago, give or take a month. Your hair was a lighter color and much longer, and you must have been wearing contact lenses." She amended her observation with the comment, "Or you're wearing them now. Anyway, your attire was quite flamboyant, and your tie was tomato red that evening. Perhaps you were in some sort of a disguise . . ." She flicked a glance at his badge. ". . . Mr. Johnson."

The man with the ugly tie flushed. His more youthful counterpart looked startled.

Viva shifted her attention to the most mature man of the trio. Tall and sturdily constructed, he wore a conservative summer-weight navy suit, subtly patterned blue-gray tie, and steel-rimmed glasses. Seated directly across from her, he met her gaze and smiled. Viva decided then that he was in charge, not because he was the oldest or because he ignored his colleague, but because he possessed a sense of humor.

"Wasn't I supposed to recognize you?" she asked, sounding as innocent as a four-year-old.

Spence winked at her and reached for her hand. Weaving his fingers through her more slender ones and mating their palms, he sank back in his chair. "Where would you like to begin?"

"How about an overview of your interest in this case, from your personal perspective, Mr. Hammond," suggested the man who hadn't spoken yet.

With a nod to him, Spence started them off. "Certainly. As I indicated during one of my conversations with a member of your staff, Miss Conrad and I are very old friends. We're also business partners now."

Removing his glasses, the older man pinched the bridge of his nose before he spoke. "Please accept my condolences, Miss Conrad. Your uncle was an exceptional man. The Justice Department lost a good friend when he passed away. I admired him a great deal."

"Thank you," Viva whispered, surprised by the compassion and genuine emotion she heard in the investigator's voice.

"Please continue," he urged, his gaze encompassing both Spence and Viva.

"Viva, as you already know, was engaged to my late stepbrother. Michael had become involved in several business deals with Daltry Renaud. Shortly after their engagement was called off, Michael died under very questionable circumstances. Both Viva and I believe that he was murdered on the orders of Daltry Renaud, although we don't know precisely why."

"Miss Conrad discovered his body, according to the police reports," asserted Mr. Johnson.

She nodded. "That's right. I also found the suicide note that Michael supposedly wrote."

"Supposedly?" chimed in the youngest of the three. "The police report specifically states that you reinforced their presumption that he wrote it. You're also quoted as saying that it reflected his state of mind prior to his death."

Viva glanced at Spence before she spoke. "It was typed, and I had no other choice."

"Why is that, Miss Conrad?" demanded Johnson.

Viva noticed and took a bit of satisfaction from

the annoyed look the older man flashed in his direction. She continued her explanation, her attention refocused on her memories. "Because Renaud called Michael's home just moments after I found his body. He made it clear to me that Spence and his daughter would be next if . . . if I compromised him in any way. I assumed then, as I assumed immediately after Michael's funeral services when Renaud approached me a second time, that he would use whatever leverage he thought he had to guarantee that I didn't speak to anyone, especially the authorities, concerning his association with Michael. He refused to believe me when I told him that I didn't know anything about their business dealings. Michael never discussed any of that with me. Unfortunately, Renaud knew that Spence and his daughter were important to me, so he guaranteed my silence by using their lives as a bargaining chip. Renaud called me an insurance policy." She hated the label, but those had been Renaud's exact words. She knew she wouldn't ever forget them.

"And his threats prompted your departure from Kentucky on the heels of Mike Hammond's death?" Johnson clarified.

"Yes," she answered. "I was desperate to eliminate any doubt in Renaud's mind about my intentions. I knew my decision was risky, especially since I suspected that Spence probably didn't believe his stepbrother had killed himself, but I assumed that his worry over Uncle Tommy's failing health and their business interests would prevent him from investigating Michael's death on his own."

"She was right," Spence confirmed, "but only up to a point. I hired a private investigator when the police closed the case, but something scared him off. I hired a second guy, but he returned my retainer three days into the job and said there wasn't any evidence that the police had overlooked. Personally, I think Renaud or his thugs got to them, but I obviously can't prove it."

The senior man shifted his gaze to Viva. "The last time I spoke to him, Tommy hinted that you wouldn't have left home unless you'd been manipulated or frightened or both."

"Tommy was the only one who knew the whole truth," she admitted. "And I asked him not to reveal it to anyone."

"He kept his promise to you, Miss Conrad," conceded the investigator.

"In his own way and only up until his death," Viva corrected him. "By leaving me the bulk of his assets, he guaranteed that Spence would find me. Uncle Tommy knew exactly what he set in motion."

"He also called me at my office in Washington a few weeks before he passed away," admitted the senior man. "We chatted about several matters of mutual interest, and near the end of our conversation he said I might hear from you before the close of the Del Mar meet."

Startled, Viva looked at Spence. "Were you aware of this?" she asked.

He shook his head. "No, but I'm fast coming to the conclusion that we've all been manipulated to one degree or another. At least Tommy's motives were honorable."

Sinking back in her chair, Viva scanned the faces of the men lined up on the opposite side of the conference table. "So, what do we do now?"

"Are you willing to make a statement on the record?" asked the youngest man.

"Of course," Viva answered. "Spence and I contacted you because we want to be of assistance to the authorities."

"Are you willing to trust the Justice Department?" pressed the senior investigator. "And are you willing to let us do our jobs?"

Viva wanted to believe that the Justice Department could and would do its job, but she knew from experience how clever Renaud could be. "I'm sure you're very competent, but Renaud is . . ." She paused, searching for the right word, a loathsome enough word to describe him.

As Viva's silence lengthened, Spence declared heatedly, "Renaud's a ruthless, self-serving murderer. I don't have any doubt that he'll kill again if he feels threatened. The bottom line here is simple: Viva is in jeopardy as long as he's not in custody."

"So are you and Emily," she whispered, worry in her eyes as she looked at him.

"You're both right," said the investigator as he

got to his feet, reached into the breast pocket of his suit, and withdrew a plastic eyeglasses case.

Viva watched his two companions stand. As he removed his steel-rimmed glasses and replaced them with a pair of dark-tinted sunglasses, he didn't say a word. Viva noticed that the other two men remained conspicuously silent. She wondered how many times the three had performed this same ritual. She also wondered what it meant.

"What exactly do you want us to do?" Viva finally managed, uncertainty obscuring her optimism that Renaud might someday be held accountable for his crimes.

"I'm asking you both to go about the business of your lives. Don't vary your routines all that much, and don't look over your shoulder every time you leave a building. In short, act as normal as possible. Renaud's made some major mistakes in recent months, and we've documented every one of them. In fact, he's been the focus of a full-scale investigation for nearly two years now." He paused, then turned to his two companions. "I'll meet you in the parking garage in five minutes."

Viva noted their reluctance to leave even though the two men silently gathered up their sample cases and made their way out of the conference room. Once the door to the room was securely closed, their superior circled around the oversize table. Spence pushed up to his feet. Viva followed suit, studying the Justice Department investigator as he paused before her.

He quietly urged, "Don't judge them too harshly. One of their co-workers died because of Renaud, so this investigation has become very personal for them."

"I think we understand the personal part better than most," Spence reminded him.

Viva saw compassion in the man's hazel eyes as his gaze moved back and forth between them. She liked him, she realized, liked his manner and his obvious intelligence.

"Of course you understand, but I'm still asking you to cooperate. You won't be disappointed if you do."

"There are notarized statements from both of us in a safe-deposit box at a Del Mar bank." Spence handed him a sealed envelope. "My attorney has the other key. If anything happens to us, we want Renaud held accountable for what he's done."

The man from Justice turned his attention to Viva. She nodded, affirming Spence's comments. She wondered then if he realized that his fatigue made him seem older. He'd looked about fifty at first glance, but now she realized that he was closer to forty. She didn't say anything, but the half smile that suddenly softened the angular lines of his face told her that he knew exactly what she was thinking.

He tucked the envelope Spence handed him into his jacket pocket. "You've been very thorough."

"So has Renaud," Spence pointed out. "He's

done a great deal of damage to our lives and to the lives of other innocent people. He needs to be stopped."

"I agree with you, Mr. Hammond."

"One more thing," Spence said, his voice as inflexible as granite. "We'll cooperate with you, but if Renaud looks like he's going to make a move against Viva, then all bets are off."

He hesitated, then admitted, "I have people assigned to Miss Conrad."

"You do?" she whispered, taken aback by the very idea that anyone, let alone a federal agent, was watching over her.

He nodded. "And to Mr. Hammond as well. The partnership horses are under the same security blanket, as is Ben Wilding, your trainer."

"You were more than a casual friend to Uncle Tommy," Viva said.

"I was," he confirmed, "but it would be best if I clarify my relationship with him at another time."

Viva nodded, wondering if she'd inadvertently tripped over a mystery somehow connected to her mother's, and Uncle Tommy's, family. She put her curiosity on a mental back burner for the time being, though.

"Now, can I inform our legal staff that you're both willing to testify in open court?" he asked.

"Yes," Viva and Spence answered simultaneously.

He appeared relieved as he removed his sunglasses and smiled at them both. "We have other witnesses against Renaud, people like you who have taken personal losses. We also have a mountain of evidence against him. We've been building this case with great care and attention to detail. Justice doesn't intend to let Renaud walk this time." After a slight pause, he confided, "If things come together as I expect them to, Renaud and his partners will be taken into custody as indictments are handed down against them in federal court on at least a dozen counts of extortion and three counts, possibly four, of first-degree murder. There will be other charges, of course, but the ones I've just mentioned are the most notable."

He extended his hand to Spence, who accepted the polite gesture. He then turned to Viva and clasped both her hands, engulfing them in his own. "I promised Tommy that you wouldn't be harmed. I won't break that promise." Releasing her, he stepped back.

"Mr. Jackson," she began, feeling a little overwhelmed as she glanced at his name tag.

"Jack Howell," he corrected.

"Mr. Howell, Michael was murdered. I didn't see it happen, but Renaud practically admitted it to me during our most recent conversation."

"I know."

Frowning, Spence clarified, "Is the Conrad estate here in San Diego under surveillance?"

"The last time we talked, Tommy gave me permission to monitor the phone lines at all of his homes. His way, I suspect, of letting your government protect you, miss, since he knew he could no longer do it himself."

She exhaled shakily. "Then you know about Renaud's most recent phone call?" Although Jack Howell smiled, Viva saw that there was no real humor or warmth in his expression.

"I've heard the tapes, and the transcripts of that particular conversation are locked in my safe. You handled yourself very well."

"I thought I'd made a mess of things," Viva admitted. "Daltry Renaud is a frightening man."

Howell jerked a nod of agreement. "I know what he's done to you, and I have a pretty good idea of the stress you've both been living under. You've been through a lot in the last fifteen months, but I'm still going to need your cooperation when we prosecute Renaud."

"We'll do everything we can," Spence promised as he slid his arm around Viva's waist and tugged her against his body.

She managed a faint smile. "Everything," Viva confirmed.

Howell withdrew a business card from his jacket pocket and handed it to Viva. "If you need help, use the number on that card." He fell silent for a brief moment, then said somberly, "A good friend of mine died on Renaud's orders, so this is personal for me too."

Viva and Spence watched in silence as Jack Howell slipped his sunglasses back onto his face, collected his sample case, and walked past them. He paused in the open doorway of the conference room. "I'll be in touch. Stay alert, both of you." He disappeared from sight a heartbeat later.

Viva turned and looked up at Spence. "I trust him. He's a good man, even if he lives an incredibly lonely life."

"Why lonely?" he asked as they strolled out of the conference room.

"Didn't you notice his eyes?"

Spence glanced at her. "I guess not."

"I did. I've seen that look in the mirror. He doesn't have much of a personal life, if any. It's a difficult way to live."

He settled his hands on her shoulders once they reached her office and stopped in front of her desk. "Things are going to be different now, Viva."

She made herself smile up at him, made herself act as though nothing remained amiss. "I hope so."

Slipping free of his loose hold, she collected her purse from a desk drawer and said a quiet prayer that Spence would express his feelings fairly soon. Not knowing made her feel vulnerable.

"You're worried about Renaud," he speculated as they departed her office and walked down the hallway to the elevator.

Viva nodded. "Very worried," she admitted, revealing only part of what weighed so heavily on her mind at the moment.

Are you in love with me? wasn't exactly the kind of question she was prepared to ask any man. And she certainly had no intention of asking Spence.

⸻❖————❖

Viva and Spence discussed Jack Howell's advice over lunch and concluded that, barring any new threats from Daltry Renaud, they would maintain their normal schedules. Viva resumed work at her office, while Spence returned to his suite at L'Auberge for a meeting with the owner of a mare he wanted to acquire for the partnership.

During the next three days, they both attended a few social events with old friends and new business partners, but they went their separate ways each night.

Viva felt uneasy about returning to the track and inadvertently drawing Renaud's attention, but her instincts told her that not attending the Pacific Classic Race would strike an even more discordant note with him. The race was considered one of the high points of the Thoroughbred season at Del Mar.

She spent the morning at her office, then drove to the track. She arrived shortly before the first race of the day, and immediately joined Spence in their reserved box at track level. Once he greeted her and showed her to her seat, he told her that Renaud was positioned only a few boxes away. She acknowledged the information with a faint smile as she accepted the glass of wine he handed her.

Butterflies dive-bombed in her stomach, so she set aside the wine. She concentrated on behaving naturally as acquaintances from Kentucky and other parts of the country assembled in the adjacent boxes. She wasn't altogether sure how she got through the afternoon, but she managed the task.

She kept her smile in place and chatted with a variety of people, deliberately projecting the image of a woman with few cares and even fewer concerns. In truth, Viva felt totally fragmented, and she longed to vent her frustration with the waiting game they were playing with Renaud by indulging in a primal scream or two.

Although she watched each race, she didn't register the fact that old friends from home owned the four-year-old colt that captured the Pacific Classic title until she saw them being photographed in the winner's circle, along with track officials, local dignitaries, the trainer, and their prize Thoroughbred with his jockey still astride him.

Spence escorted Viva to valet parking after the final race of the day. She half envied, half resented his composure. Viva suspected that she looked as frayed around the edges as she felt. As she got into her vehicle and adjusted her seat belt, he leaned down to kiss her cheek.

"I'll call you later," he promised before he straightened and eased shut the door of her car. Once she lowered the window, he gave her a reassuring smile. "Drive carefully, partner."

She nodded, then glanced past him and spotted Daltry Renaud. When he met her gaze and inclined his head in his version of a greeting, she gave him a brief but polite smile. She started her car and joined the flow of traffic headed out of the race-track parking facility, but her respiration remained uneven for several minutes.

Following stops at the grocery store and the dry cleaners, she walked into the kitchen of the estate a few hours later. The phone rang. Assuming it was Spence, Viva answered it after dropping her purse and the grocery sack on the kitchen counter.

"How are you today, Miss Conrad?"

"All right," she said, surprised to hear Jack Howell's voice.

"As far as I'm concerned, you're doing just fine."

She exhaled shallowly before she spoke. "Thank you, but I'm a little on edge."

"That's understandable," he assured her. "I gather that tomorrow is an important day for Oak-brook Farm."

"Yes, it is. Anticipation is running in the first race of the day."

He observed, "After taking the Belmont Stakes and the Preakness, she looks well-positioned to win the Ramona Handicap. Some of the veteran handi-cappers at the track are comparing her to Genuine Risk."

Viva smiled, this time with real pleasure. "Spence and I share their optimism. And the purse is nothing to sneeze at, either."

He chuckled. "You'll be there?"

"Shouldn't I?" she asked, gripping the receiver

because something in his voice hinted that she might want to reevaluate her decision.

"You'll want to attend, Viva. It promises to be a very eventful day," he said quietly.

Jack Howell said nothing else. She absently listened to the dial tone for several seconds after he severed the connection. Once she recradled the receiver, she sank into the nearest chair until she stopped shaking.

After going over his words and factoring into the equation his tone of voice, Viva thought she understood his message. Tomorrow would be a pivotal day in all of their lives.

Determined to master her growing anxiety, she reached for the telephone, dialed Spence's pager number, and left a message on his voice mail that she felt confident he would understand: "The pharmacy reps called to wish us luck with Anticipation."

Viva and Spence spoke briefly that night, but they avoided comments that didn't relate to their partnership interests. As she drifted off to sleep shortly after midnight, Viva prayed for an end to the tension and fear that had dominated her life for so long. She added a second plea for some hint from Spence about his feelings for her. Was she the only one who'd fallen in love?

Anticipation's big day dawned bright and sunny. Once again, Viva kept to her routine. She arrived early at the office, participated in two meetings with clinic staffers, and then drove up to Del Mar at lunchtime. She made her way through the crowds to the saddling paddock in order to join Spence, Anticipation, the jockey selected to ride her, and Ben Wilding, the trainer.

Like Spence, she wore a deep green linen jacket and white linen trousers, the green and white of their clothing reflecting the approved silks worn by their jockey and the signature colors of Oakbrook Farm. While Ben accompanied Anticipation and her jockey to the starting gate, Viva and Spence adjourned to their reserved box.

Several friends wished them well in the hectic moments before the race started, but she barely heard their comments. She'd spotted Daltry Renaud and two men who looked vaguely familiar in Renaud's reserved box. Positioned directly behind them in the aisle were two unsavory-looking characters. She shivered when she noticed the emotionless quality of their facial expressions.

Viva flinched when Spence took her hand. She met his gaze.

"Relax," he urged.

She nodded, her eyes huge with fear. She couldn't get the nightmarish images of Michael's death out of her mind. "I'm okay," she insisted.

"Howell and his people are here. Let's just watch our girl win, all right?"

Viva squared her shoulders as Spence squeezed her hand and then released it. She immediately missed his touch.

The look he gave her said that he wanted to do much more than just hold her hand. He winked at her, then mouthed the word, "Later."

The announcer's voice sounded over the public-address system to announce the start of the race. Tension hummed in the salt-laden air rolling in from the ocean. Like the thousands of people in attendance, Viva and Spence surged to their feet and focused on the track.

To Viva's delight, Anticipation left her competition in her dust the instant she sprang free of the starting gate. The crowd in the grandstands roared their approval as she thundered down the dirt track under the capable guidance of her experienced jockey.

Anticipation won the six-furlong race in record time.

Although she'd expected the filly to take the race, Viva experienced a moment of pure delight that couldn't be tainted by the Daltry Renauds of the world. Spence shouted his pleasure that Anticipation crossed the finish line well in front of the other Thoroughbreds on the track. He enveloped Viva in a bear hug, and swung her around in a circle several times before lowering her to the ground.

For a few brief seconds she felt the euphoria of triumph as it flooded her consciousness. Once she regained her footing, Spence seized her hand.

Together, they hurried down to the winner's circle. In the madness that ensued, Viva and Spence were bombarded with congratulatory shouts from friends and strangers alike. Ben met them in the winner's circle, his British reserve absent as he grinned broadly, shook hands with Spence, and then embraced Viva.

With Anticipation and her jockey taking center stage, the three gathered around the Thoroughbred at the request of the photographer who'd accompanied track officials to the winner's circle. Smiling, Viva scanned the cheering crowd, but her gaze snagged on one section of reserved seating in particular.

Riveted by the unfolding drama that had just begun to play itself out, she felt a chill sweep across her soul. She stared, unable to drag her gaze from the sight of Jack Howell and a contingent of personnel from the Justice Department as they converged on Daltry Renaud and his companions. Renaud's outrage showed in his face. A scuffle ensued, but Renaud, his associates, and the bodyguards standing in the aisle were instantly outmanned and outgunned.

Not quite believing her eyes, Viva witnessed the arrest of the man who'd caused death and trauma to so many. She started to weep silently, the relief she felt like a tide moving over her in slow motion as, all around her, excitement reigned supreme in both the grandstands and in the chaos still taking place in the winner's circle. Few people even noticed the downfall of Daltry Renaud.

Startled when Spence gripped her hand, Viva looked at him. His warm touch and her awareness of his presence finally shattered the surreal spell that had fallen over her.

"How are you doing?" he asked as he leaned down to be heard above the noise.

"Renaud . . ." She choked and couldn't finish the sentence.

"I saw it, too, little one."

"It's finally over," she whispered, tears still streaming down her face. "He's in custody."

"Come here," he said as he gathered her into his arms and held her.

She found instant comfort in his embrace. "I'm almost afraid to believe what I just saw happen." Trembling, she held on to him with all the strength she possessed. "I feel as if we've been living on a roller coaster."

"Believe it, little one. The bastard is about to be history."

She didn't protest when Spence guided her out of the winner's circle, up a flight of stairs, and along a corridor situated behind the grandstand seating area. He paused, his arm sliding around her waist, and tapped on the door.

Jack Howell pulled it open and stepped aside. As soon as they walked inside, he secured the door and faced them. "The indictments came down this morning. Renaud and his buddies are in the custody of the federal government, their assets are frozen by order of a federal magistrate, and they'll be arraigned in Washington within forty-eight hours."

"Thank God," Viva said breathlessly.

Jack smiled. "Justice did some of the work."

"More than I thought you could," Spence admitted as the two men shook hands. He tightened his hold on Viva before he spoke again. "Do we need security for Viva and Emily?"

Jack sobered. "It's already arranged, although I'm not really expecting any problems. This is a case of rendering the snake useless by cutting off his head."

"Thank you," Viva said, feeling more composed.

Jack shook his head, the negative gesture emphatic. "Your cooperation and your willingness to testify put me in your debt, Viva."

She studied him and was struck yet again by the familiarity of his eyes, not just his overall physical construction. "Are we related?" Viva asked.

Spence gave her a startled look.

Jack hesitated, then remarked, "You're even more observant than I suspected."

"We are, aren't we?"

Jack Howell nodded. "Tommy Conrad was my father. I found out a few years ago."

"We're cousins!" she exclaimed. "That's wonderful."

He half smiled. "I wasn't sure how you'd react."

"We're family, and I'm delighted."

He shrugged. "Wait'll you get to know me. You might change your mind."

She beamed. "I doubt that."

"What about Michael?" Spence asked. "Would

he have been on the receiving end of some of those indictments if he'd lived?"

Jack Howell's features tightened. "Mike Hammond worked for me at Justice. He was a deep-cover investigator."

Relieved and shocked at the same time, Viva's eyes widened. "He's the friend you mentioned when we talked the first time."

Jack nodded. "He was our friend and a part of our team. We don't know exactly how, but Renaud discovered the connection and had him executed."

Stunned, Viva fell silent as waves of shock moved through her. Beside her, Spence struggled for several moments with his emotions before he quietly said, "Thank you for telling us."

"I couldn't until now." Jack walked over to a briefcase positioned atop a desk that had been shoved up against a wall in the windowless room. He withdrew a leather-bound volume. "Mike wanted you to have his personal journal. It explains a lot, the choices he's made over the years and his feelings about those choices."

Spence ground his jaws together for a few seconds after Jack handed him the journal. He opened his mouth to speak, but he closed it again without saying a word.

Viva knew he needed to collect himself, so she asked, "Do you need us for anything else today?" She also needed a reprieve from everything surrounding Daltry Renaud.

Jack shook his head. "Why don't we set up a

meeting once you've both had time to relax and regroup? Get on with your lives, but be aware that there are people from Justice monitoring your activities twenty-four hours a day. They won't intrude, but they'll be handy if anything odd crops up."

Spence and Viva walked to the door, but Viva turned and smiled. "Welcome to the family, cousin."

Jack Howell smiled. "Thanks, cousin."

"We need to talk about family stuff."

"You've got yourself a deal." His smile broadened to a full-fledged grin.

"You should do that more often," Viva said, referring to his amused expression. "You look like Uncle Tommy when he was in his prime. That's a compliment, by the way," she added.

Jack glanced at Spence. "She must be hell on wheels some of the time."

Spence laughed. "No kidding." Then he hustled a protesting Viva out of the small office.

ELEVEN

Spence frowned as he watched Viva pace the balcony. Instead of relaxing now that Renaud had been taken into custody, she'd grown progressively more skittish in the hours since his arrest.

She'd picked at her food when they'd stopped for a light supper at a bayside restaurant, and his repeated attempts to engage her in conversation had failed. He'd managed to keep his worry and frustration at bay until now, but he knew his own temperament well enough to realize that his patience was nearing an end.

Once they returned to the hilltop estate, he'd used the study phone to make several phone calls while Viva showered and then dressed in a flowing silk caftan. Rather than seeking him out after freshening up, she'd avoided him, which set his nerves on edge even more. He eventually found her on the balcony, and they'd watched the sun sink to the horizon seated on opposite sides of the table and in total silence.

Spence didn't want to crowd her. He knew how difficult the last fifteen months had been for her, but he concluded that giving her time to unwind had done little in the way of lessening her tension. If anything, it had heightened it, at least from his perspective.

Abandoning his chair on the balcony when he finally exhausted what little patience he possessed, Spence strolled to the railing after Viva ceased her pacing and paused there.

"When are you coming home?" he asked as he stood beside her.

She didn't meet his gaze. "I'm not really sure."

Her response to his question didn't really surprise him. She'd become a master at evasive answers, he realized with a sinking heart. "Why?"

Viva shrugged as she stared at the twinkling lights of the San Diego skyline. "I have a lot going on at the clinic." She slowly turned to look at him. "It doesn't really matter where I live."

"Of course, it matters."

She shook her head. "No, it doesn't. Besides, we're still in limbo as far as Renaud is concerned."

"Jack's case against him is solid enough, from what he's said, to put the guy away forever."

"I don't really want to talk about this right now, Spence." She pushed away from the railing.

He caught her arm before she could move past him. "Running again, little one?"

"Just going into the kitchen."

Despite her mild tone of voice, he didn't miss the undercurrent of wariness in her words. "Look at me," he said quietly.

When she did, Spence felt as if he'd been gut-punched. "Tell me what's going on in your head."

"I can't. At least, not right now."

When she tried to free herself, he locked his hands around her wrists and held her still. Searching her face, he saw more than sadness. He saw resignation and defeat, and he needed to understand the cause, so he insisted, "Now."

"Don't pressure me," she whispered as she tried to evade his hold. She failed, and her shoulders slumped.

Spence very carefully drew her forward, treating her as though she might shatter if he moved too quickly or aggressively. "You haven't been yourself since we left the racetrack. What's wrong?"

She trembled as he wrapped his arms around her and aligned their bodies. "Nothing's wrong," she told him in a subdued voice. "I just have a lot on my mind."

"Are you really that worried about Renaud?"

She nodded, then rested her forehead against his shoulder. "I'm very worried. He hasn't even been arraigned yet. A lot can happen."

"What else is bothering you?"

"Nothing," she said too quickly.

"You're lying to me, and I want to know why."

Viva stiffened. "Let go of me."

Spence complied with her demand, then watched her make her way across the balcony and into the kitchen. He followed her, more out of instinct than by design. He watched her pour a few inches of chardonnay into her wineglass before she turned to look at him.

His gaze dipped, and he saw more evidence of her tension in her white-knuckled grip on the glass she held. His own anxiety spiking, he told himself not to overreact to her behavior or her mood, but he couldn't get past the notion that she was deliberately shutting him out. He intended to know why, and he didn't plan on waiting very long for an explanation.

"I have commitments here that I can't walk away from," she reminded him.

"You'll need to give your notice and train your replacement," he said, striving for a reasonable tone as he tried to address the concerns he thought she might have about leaving southern California and returning home. "I don't have a problem with that, especially if it'll free you up for more important things."

"More important things?" she repeated.

"Yeah, like our business relationship for starters."

"That's probably a moot point now."

He frowned. "Explain."

"Jack Howell. Uncle Tommy's son and his rightful heir. Remember him?"

"Jack's not an issue."

"Of course he's an issue. He has a legitimate claim on Tommy's estate. I don't have a problem with that. No problem at all. It would certainly simplify my life."

"I said he's not an issue." His voice contained the sharpness of a new razor blade. "He never was, and he never will be."

"How can you be so sure?"

"I've spoken to Harlan."

"And?"

"And Tommy took care of Jack before he died. Your uncle had extensive holdings. Our partnership was just one piece of the pie. Jack is set for life. Probably several lifetimes, now that I think about it. Tommy also took steps to acknowledge their relationship legally."

Viva smiled. "I'm glad they found each other. Did Harlan give you any of the details about their relationship or why it took them so long to be reunited?"

"No, but I suspect that Jack eventually will."

"I like him."

"Me, too, but why don't we get back to the real point of this entire conversation?"

"Which is?" she said, her expression instantly guarded.

"Our marriage, which will not be bicoastal."

She stared at him. "Marriage?"

He nodded.

"We're not getting married," she announced,

her chin lifting and giving her a stubborn look that Spence instantly recognized.

"We're partners, so it makes sense to go the whole nine yards."

"That's a merger, not a marriage, and I'm definitely not interested."

Blue eyes flashing, she walked past him and out of the kitchen. She marched down the hallway to her bedroom. He followed her, catching the door before it slammed in his face. Approaching her, he relieved her of the wineglass she carried and placed it on the bureau. He smiled at the outraged expression on her face as he walked back to her.

"I want you to leave," she said as she vibrated with an inner tension that brought a flush to her skin.

Spence nodded, scooped her up before she drew her next breath, and dropped her onto the center of her bed.

She lurched up to a kneeling position and glared at him as he shed his clothing in record time. "Are you deaf?"

He advanced on her, gently took her shoulders, and toppled her onto her back. Leaning over her, he efficiently jerked the front of her caftan apart, sending dozens of buttons flying every which way, then stripped it off her body.

"What do you think you're doing?" she demanded as she glared up at him.

He watched her nipples tighten into mauve nuggets that invited his mouth. "Easing your tension," he announced in a matter-of-fact tone, despite the heat flooding his loins and engorging his sex. He came down over her, his hips lodging between her thighs, his upper body weight braced by his arms. "As sexist as that probably sounds."

She squirmed, trying to free herself, and a sound of fury burst out of her when she failed to budge him.

"What about our children?"

She stilled instantly. "What children?"

"The ones we're going to have. I think they should have my name, don't you?"

"We're not getting married, so it doesn't matter one way or another."

"Tell me again why you ended your engagement to Michael."

She closed her eyes, but she answered him in a tight little voice. "I don't like to repeat myself."

Spence smothered the smile that threatened. He knew by the look on her face that she wanted to hit something. Preferably him. "Humor me, Viva."

"Forget it. I'm not in the mood to play word games with you."

"You're in love with me, Viva."

She shot a furious look at him. "Don't throw that in my face. It was obviously an error in judgment on my part. I'll get over it. Quickly, I assure you."

His expression serious, Spence cradled her face between his broad-palmed hands. "Please don't ever get over it."

She cocked her head to one side, searching his features with curious eyes. "Give me one good reason," she said, sounding less angry now.

"I love you."

She mulled that over.

He fought for and found the patience to go the distance with her.

"We're friends. People love their friends."

"We're also lovers," he added.

She nodded. "We were."

"We are, and we always will be."

"Don't be so sure of yourself."

"I am sure. I've fallen in love with you," he said after several quiet seconds filled with the deafening sound of his hammering heart. "Didn't you know that?"

"I didn't know," she whispered, looking shocked.

"Does it make a difference?"

"Why? I mean, why are you in love with me?"

He chuckled. He would never understand the way a woman's mind worked. His common sense assured him that he was better off not knowing. "Do I have to have a reason?"

"Absolutely." Her vivid blue eyes sparkled with mischief.

"I just know that I fell in love with you, and I'll be damned if I'll justify what I feel."

"You sound angry."

"I am. With you for not realizing how I feel about you."

"I don't read minds, Spence."

"Neither do I."

"At least I was honest," she reminded him in her own defense.

"Only when I forced you to be."

"I don't want to argue."

"What do you want?"

She shifted her hips. Pure invitation. "You."

He bit back the groan wedged in his throat. His flesh, already hard and poised at the entrance to her body, surged with response, though. He ached to be inside of her, but he held back. "Persuasive," he remarked.

She smiled.

"You look more relaxed now," he observed after leaning down to sample in a leisurely fashion the heated flavors of her mouth. "You taste good too."

Viva stroked him from shoulders to hips, then brought her hands up to tangle her fingers at his nape. "You're sure you're in love with me?"

He nodded, the strain of holding back evident in the angular lines of his hard-featured face. "I've never been more sure of anything in my life. And I'm still waiting for an answer from you."

She gave him an uncertain look. "Did you ask a question?"

He hadn't, he realized. He'd told her. "Will you marry me, Viva Conrad?"

"Yes."

"Will you make babies with me?"

Tears filled her eyes, overflowed, and spilled free. She nodded.

"Will you get old with me? And will you always love me?"

"Yes, yes, yes!" she exclaimed, hugging him with all of her strength.

Spence eased back a few moments later to find her still weeping silently. "Why are you crying?"

She smiled through her tears. "I'm happy."

Shaking his head in amazement, he gathered her close and rolled onto his back. Viva wound up sprawled across his muscular torso. She shifted suddenly, joining their bodies in the ultimate expression of physical love. She moaned softly as she accustomed herself to Spence's pulsing strength, then opened her eyes to look at him. "I love you, Spencer Hammond. I will always love you."

"Jack was right," he muttered as she shimmied her hips in her own unique dance of love in the moments that followed her declaration. The eroticism of her nature tantalized him in ways he couldn't even begin to describe, so he didn't try for eloquence when he finally managed to speak. "You're hell on wheels, little one."

As Viva flowed down across his chest, Spence embraced her, pledging his heart to her for the rest of his life. They made love with a deliberateness that left them breathless as their bodies, hearts, and souls mated forever.

THE EDITORS' CORNER

It's hot in the city! And in the country. And in the North. And in the South. And in the mountains. And at the seashore. And . . . well, you get the picture. It's just plain hot! Don't worry though, Loveswept's September loot of books will match the sultry weather out there. Even the air conditioner won't stop these characters from sizzling right off the pages and into your homes!

Devlin Sinclair and Gabrielle Rousseau are walking **ON THIN ICE**, LOVESWEPT #850, Eve Gaddy's novel about two attorneys bent on taking on the world and each other. Thrown together through no wish of their own, Devlin and Gabrielle must defend a reputed crime boss—a case that could ultimately make their careers, involving a man who could ultimately ruin Gabrielle's life. Devlin knew there was more to his sinfully gorgeous partner, especially since he accidentally bumped into her in the Midnight and Lace Lingerie shop! Annoyed that Devlin looked as if he'd guessed her wildest secrets, Gabrielle had to struggle not to melt when the charming rogue called her beautiful. But sometimes, in the heat of denial, one can discover heat of another kind. Eve Gaddy's romantic adventure pairs a fallen angel with a man who's her match in all things sensual and judicial!

In **AFTERGLOW,** LOVESWEPT #851 by Loveswept favorite Faye Hughes, professional treasure hunter Sean Kilpatrick is about to meet her match when she joins forces with Dalton Gregory in the search for a legendary cache of gold, silver, and priceless jewels buried somewhere on Gregory land. When Dalton comes to town to oust Sean, who he's sure is just a slick huckster on the make, he finds a copper-haired beauty whose enthusiasm for the project quickly becomes infectious. Sean is stunned by her intense attraction to this gorgeous, yet conservative history professor, but when he agrees to help chase a fortune, close quarters may not be all that they share. Spending more time together only accentuates the slow burn that is raging into a steady afterglow. Faye Hughes tempts readers with the ultimate treasure hunt in a tantalizingly steamy romantic romp!

Cheryln Biggs tells a deliciously unpredictable tale about the **GUNSLINGER'S LADY,** LOVESWEPT #852. There's a new girl in town in Tombstone, Arizona, and Jack Ringo aims to find out just what she's doing sprawled in his cactus patch dressed up in petticoats—especially since the Old West Festival doesn't start until tomorrow! Kate Holliday can't understand why Johnny Ringo is dressed up in strange clothes and without his guns, but the man was definitely as dangerously handsome as ever! Jack is quickly bewitched by Kate's mystery, frustrated at her existence, and inflamed by the heated passion of a woman who may disappear with the dawn. Adrift in a world she'd never imagined, uncertain of all but one man's need, can a sassy adventuress find her future in the arms of a man who couldn't guarantee the coming of tomorrow? Cheryln Biggs delivers a timeless love story that dabbles in destiny and breaks all the rules!

Loveswept newcomer Pat Van Wie adds to our lineup of delectable September romances **RUNNING FOR COVER,** LOVESWEPT #853. When Deputy Marshal Kyle Munroe shows up at Jennifer Brooks's classroom door complete with an entourage, Jenny knows that her time of peace and security is long gone. Jenny is reluctant to trust the man who had once shunned all she had to offer, but deep down she knows that Kyle may very well be the only one she can truly count on. Threats against her father's life also put hers in danger and the reluctant pair go into hiding . . . until betrayal catapults them into a desperate flight. And once again, Kyle and Jenny are faced with the same decisions, whether to find safety and love together, or shadows and sadness apart. Sizzling with sexual tension and the breathless thrill of love on the run, Pat Van Wie's first Loveswept explores the joy and heartache of a desire too strong to subdue.

Happy reading!

With warmest regards,

Shauna Summers   *Joy Abella*

Shauna Summers   Joy Abella

Editor   Administrative Editor

P.S. Look for these Bantam women's fiction titles coming in August. *New York Times* bestseller Tami Hoag's breathtakingly sensual novel, **DARK PARADISE**, is filled with heart-stopping suspense and shocking passion. Marilee Jennings is drawn to a man as hard and untamable as the land he loves, and to a town steeped in secrets—where a killer lurks. Another *New York Times* bestselling author, Betina Krahn, is back with **THE MERMAID**, a tale of a woman ahead of her time and an academic who must decide if he will risk everything he holds dear to side with the Lady Mermaid. Dubbed the queen of romantic adventure by *Affaire de Coeur*, Katherine O'Neal returns with **BRIDE OF DANGER**, her most spellbinding—and irresistible—novel yet! Night after night, Mylene charmed the secrets out of men's souls, and not one suspected that she was a spy devoted to the cause of freedom. Until the evening she came face-to-face with the mysterious Lord Whitney, a man who will ask her to betray everything she's ever believed in. And immediately following this page, preview the Bantam women's fiction titles on sale in July.

Don't miss these extraordinary books
by your favorite Bantam authors

On sale in July:

THE SILVER ROSE
by Jane Feather

A PLACE TO CALL HOME
by Deborah Smith

The newest novel in the enthralling,
passionate Charm Bracelet Trilogy . . .

"Jane Feather is an accomplished
storyteller . . . rare and wonderful."
—*Daily News of Los Angeles*

THE SILVER ROSE
by Jane Feather
author of *The Diamond Slipper*

*Like the rose in the haunting tale of "Beauty and the
Beast," a silver rose on a charm bracelet brings together a
young woman and a battle-scarred lord . . . Ariel
Ravenspeare has been taught to loathe the earl of
Hawkesmoor and everything he represents. Their two
families have been sworn enemies for generations. But it's
one thing to hate him, and another to play the part
her vicious brothers have written for her—trapping
Hawkesmoor into a marriage that will destroy him, using
herself as bait. Forced into the marriage, Ariel will find
her new husband unexpectedly difficult to manipulate, as
well as surprisingly—and powerfully—attractive. But
beneath the passion lurks the strand of a long-hidden
secret . . . a secret embodied in a sparkling silver rose.*

Ranulf stood at the door to the Great Hall. He stared
out over the thronged courtyard, and when he saw
Ariel appear from the direction of the stables, he de-

scended the steps and moved purposefully toward her. She was weaving her way through the crowd, the dogs at her heels, a preoccupied frown on her face.

"Just where the hell have you been?" Ranulf demanded in a low voice, grabbing her arm above the elbow. The dogs growled but for once he ignored them. "How dare you vanish without a word to anyone! Where have you been? Answer me!" He shook her arm. The dogs growled again, a deep-throated warning. Ranulf turned on them with a foul oath, but he released his hold.

"Why should it matter where I've been?" Ariel answered. "I'm back now."

"Dressed like some homespun peasant's wife," her brother gritted through compressed lips. "Look at you. You had money to clothe yourself properly for your bridal celebrations, and you go around in an old riding habit that looks as if it's been dragged through a haystack. And your boots are worn through."

Ariel glanced down at her broadcloth skirts. Straw and mud clung to them, and her boots, while not exactly worn through, were certainly shabby and unpolished. She had been so uncomfortable dressing under the amused eye of her bridegroom that morning that she had grabbed what came to hand and given no thought to the occasion.

"I trust you have passed a pleasant morning, my wife." Simon's easy tones broke into Ranulf's renewed diatribe. The earl of Hawkesmoor had approached through the crowd so quietly that neither Ranulf nor his sister had noticed him. Ariel looked up with a flashing smile that betrayed her relief at his interruption.

"I went for a drive in the gig. Forgive me for

staying out overlong, but I drove farther than I'd thought to without noticing the time."

"Aye, it's a fine way to do honor to your husband," Ranulf snapped. "To appear clad like a serving wench who's been rolling in the hay. I'll not have it said that the earl of Ravenspeare's sister goes about like a tavern doxy—"

"Oh, come now, Ravenspeare!" Simon again interrupted Ranulf's rising tirade. "You do even less honor to your name by reviling your sister so publicly." Ariel flushed to the roots of her hair, more embarrassed by her husband's defense than by her brother's castigation.

"Your wife's appearance does not reflect upon the Hawkesmoor name, then?" Ranulf's tone was full of sardonic mockery. "But perhaps Hawkesmoors are less nice in their standards."

"From what I've seen of your hospitality so far, Ravenspeare, I take leave to doubt that," Simon responded smoothly, not a flicker of emotion in his eyes. He turned to Ariel, who was still standing beside him, wrestling with anger and chagrin. "However, I take your point, Ravenspeare. It is for a husband to correct his wife, not her brother.

"You are perhaps a little untidy, my dear. Maybe you should settle this matter by changing into a habit that will reflect well upon both our houses. I am certain the shooting party can wait a few minutes."

Ariel turned and left without a word. She kept her head lowered, her hood drawn up to hide her scarlet cheeks. It was one of her most tormenting weaknesses. Her skin was so fair and all her life she had blushed at the slightest provocation, sometimes even without good reason. She was always mortified at her obvious embarrassment, and the situation would be impossibly magnified.

Why had Simon interfered? Ranulf's insulting rebukes ran off her like water on oiled leather. By seeming to take her part, the Hawkesmoor had made a mountain out of a molehill. But then, he hadn't really taken her part. He had sent her away to change as if she were a grubby child appearing unwashed at the dinner table.

However, when she took a look at herself in the glass in her chamber, she was forced to admit that both men had had a point. Her hair was a windwhipped tangle, her face was smudged with dust from her drive through the Fen blow, and her old broadcloth riding habit was thick with dust, the skirts caked with mud. But she'd had more important matters to attend to than her appearance, she muttered crossly, tugging at buttons and hooks.

Clad in just her shift, she washed her face and sponged her arms and neck, before letting down her hair. Throwing it forward over her face, she bent her head low and began to brush out the tangles. She was still muttering to herself behind the honeyed curtain when her husband spoke from the door.

"Your brothers' guests grow restless. I don't have much skill as a ladies' maid but perhaps I can help you."

Ariel raised her head abruptly, tossing back the glowing mane of hair. Her cheeks were pink with her efforts with the hairbrush and a renewed surge of annoyance.

The hounds greeted the new arrival with thumping tails. Their mistress, however, regarded the earl with a fulminating glare. "I have no need of assistance, my lord. And it's very discourteous to barge into my chamber without so much as a knock."

"Forgive me, but the door was ajar." His tone carelessly dismissed her objection. He closed the door on his words and surveyed her with his crooked little smile. "Besides, a wife's bedchamber is usually not barred to her husband."

"So you've already made clear, my lord," Ariel said tightly. "And I suppose it follows that a wife has no rights to privacy."

"Not necessarily." He limped forward and took the brush from her hand. "Sit." A hand on her shoulder pushed her down to the dresser stool. He began to draw the brush through the thick springy locks with strong, rhythmic strokes. "I've longed to do this since I saw you yesterday, waiting for me in the courtyard, with your hat under your arm. The sun was catching these light gold streaks in your hair. They're quite delightful." He lifted a strand that stood out much paler against the rich dark honey.

Ariel glanced at his face in the mirror. He was smiling to himself, his eyes filled with a sensual pleasure, his face, riven by the jagged scar, somehow softened as if this hair brushing were the act of a lover. She noticed how his hands, large and callused though they were, had an elegance, almost a delicacy to them. She had the urge to reach for those hands, to lay her cheek against them. A shiver ran through her.

"You're cold," he said immediately, laying down the brush. "The fire is dying." He turned to the hearth and with deft efficiency poked it back to blazing life, throwing on fresh logs. "Come now, you must make haste with your dressing before you catch cold." He limped to the armoire. "Will you wear the habit you wore yesterday? The crimson velvet suited you well." He drew out the garment as he spoke, and looked over at the sparse contents of the armoire. "You appear to have a very limited wardrobe, Ariel."

"I have little need of finery in the Fens," she stated, almost snatching the habit from him. "The life I lead doesn't lend itself to silks and velvets."

"The life you've led until now," he corrected thoughtfully, leaning against the bedpost, arms folded, as he watched her dress. "As the countess of Hawkesmoor, you will take your place at court, and in county society, I trust. The Hawkesmoors have always been active in our community of the Fens."

Unlike the lords of Ravenspeare. The local community was more inclined to hide from them than seek their aid. But neither of them spoke this shared thought.

Ariel fumbled with the tiny pearl buttons of her shirt. Her fingers were suddenly all thumbs. He sounded so assured, but she knew that she would never take her place at court or anywhere else as the wife of this man, whatever happened.

"Your hands must be freezing." He moved her fumbling fingers aside and began to slip the tiny buttons into the braided loops that fastened them. His hands brushed her breasts and her breath caught. His fingers stopped their work and she felt her nipples harden against the fine linen of her shift as goose bumps lifted on her skin. Then abruptly his hands dropped from her and he stepped back, his face suddenly closed.

She turned aside to pick up her skirt, stepping into it, fastening the hooks at her waist, trying to hide the trembling of her fingers, keeping her head lowered and averted until the hot flush died down on her creamy cheeks.

If only he would go away now. But he remained leaning against the bedpost.

She felt his eyes on her, following her every move, and that lingering sensuality in his gaze made her blood race. Even the simple act of pulling on her boots was invested with a curious voluptuousness under the intentness of his sea blue eyes. The man was ugly as sin, and yet she had never felt more powerfully attracted to anyone.

A new novel from one of the most
appealing voices in Southern fiction . . .

"A uniquely significant voice in contemporary
women's fiction."
—*Romantic Times*

A PLACE TO CALL HOME

by Deborah Smith

author of *Silk and Stone*

Deborah Smith offers an irresistible Southern saga that celebrates a sprawling, sometimes eccentric Georgia family and the daughter at the center of their hearts. Twenty years ago, Claire Maloney was the willful, pampered child of the town's most respected family, but that didn't stop her from befriending Roan Sullivan, a fierce, motherless boy who lived in a rusted-out trailer amid junked cars. No one in Dunderry—least of all Claire's family—could understand the attraction. But Roan and Claire belonged together . . . until the dark afternoon when violence and terror overtook them and Roan disappeared from Claire's life. Now, two decades later, Claire is adrift and the Maloneys are still hoping the past can be buried under the rich Southern soil . . .

I planned to be the kind of old Southern lady who talks to her tomato plants and buys sweaters for her cats. I'd just turned thirty, but I was already sizing up where I'd been and where I was headed. So I knew that when I was old I'd be deliberately *peculiar*. I'd wear bright red lipstick and tell embarrassing true stories about my family, and people would say, "I heard she was always a little funny, if you know what I mean."

They wouldn't understand why, and I didn't intend to tell them. I thought I'd sit in a rocking chair on the porch of some fake-antebellum nursing home for decrepit journalists, get drunk on bourbon and Coca-Cola, and cry over Roan Sullivan. I was only ten the last time I saw him, and he was fifteen, and twenty years had passed since then, but I'd never forgotten him and knew I never would.

"I'd like to believe life turned out well for Roanie," Mama said periodically, and Daddy nodded without meeting her eyes, and they dropped the subject. They felt guilty about the part they'd played in driving Roan away, and they knew I couldn't forgive them for it. He was one of the disappointments between them and me, which was saying a lot, since I'd felt like such a helpless failure when they brought me home from the hospital last spring.

My two oldest brothers, Josh and Brady, didn't speak about Roan at all. They were away at college during most of the Roan Sullivan era in our family. But my two other brothers remembered him each time they came back from a hunting trip with a prize buck. "It can't hold a candle to the one Roan Sullivan shot when we were kids," Evan always said to Hop. "Nope," Hop agreed with a mournful sigh. "That buck was a king." Evan and Hop measured regret in terms of antlers.

As for the rest of the family—Daddy's side, Mama's side, merged halves of a family tree so large and complex and deeply rooted it looked like an overgrown oak to strangers—Roan Sullivan was only a fading reflection in the mirror of their biases and regrets and sympathies. How they remembered him depended on how they saw themselves and our world back then, and most of them had turned that painful memory to the wall.

But he and I were a permanent fixture in local history, as vivid and tragic as anything could be in a small Georgia community isolated in the lap of the mountains, where people hoard sad stories as carefully as their great-grandmothers' china. My great-grandmother's glassware and china service, by the way, were packed in a crate in Mama and Daddy's attic. Mama had this wistful little hope that I'd use it someday, that her only girl among five children would magically and belatedly blossom into the kind of woman who set a table with china instead of plastic.

There was hope for that. But what happened to Roan Sullivan and me changed my life and changed my family. Because of him we saw ourselves as we were, made of the kindness and cruelty that bond people together by blood, marriage, and time. I tried to save him and he ended up saving me. He might have been dead for twenty years—I didn't know then—but I knew I'd come full circle because of him: I would always wait for him to come back, too.

The hardest memories are the pieces of what might have been.

On sale in August:

DARK PARADISE
by Tami Hoag

THE MERMAID
by Betina Krahn

BRIDE OF DANGER
by Katherine O'Neal

The enchanting wit of *New York Times* bestseller

BETINA KRAHN

"Krahn has a delightful, smart touch."
—*Publishers Weekly*

THE PERFECT MISTRESS
___56523-0 $5.99/$7.99 Canada

THE LAST BACHELOR
___56522-2 $5.99/$7.50 Canada

THE UNLIKELY ANGEL
___56524-9 $5.99/$7.99 Canada